T0147611

Hagon's Bluff

Buck Fisher

iUniverse, Inc.
New York Bloomington

Hagon's Bluff

iUniverse books may be ordered through booksellers or by contacting:

iUniverse
1663 Liberty Drive
Bloomington, IN 47403
www.iuniverse.com
1-800-Authors (1-800-288-4677)

ISBN: 978-1-4502-4002-4 (pbk)
ISBN: 978-1-4502-4003-1 (ebk)

Printed in the United States of America

iUniverse rev. date: 7/14/2010

1

The middle of the afternoon on May fifteenth William Bradshaw died in his hospital room. That was the worst day of Angie's life. William had been sick with cancer for over a year unable to work. He was thirty-five years old leaving behind his wife Angie, and his two children, Bryon and Amy. Bryon was twelve and Amy was ten years old, and they missed their father very much.

Angie sat around the house trying to figure out what she was going to do with her life after the funeral. May twenty-third the phone kept ringing and she tried to ignore the ringing. This was Monday, and the kids were in school. They only had a week of school left. While they were in school, she had some time to think over things. Irritated she reached over and picked up the phone receiver.

"Hello," she said trying not to sound irritated.

A man's voice came over the phone. "I'd like to talk to Angie Bradshaw."

"I'm Angie," she replied.

"I'm so sorry to hear about your loss Mrs.Bradshaw. I can call back later if this is a bad time. This matter at hand needs to be resolved as soon as possible," he told her.

"What matter is that?" she inquired.

"Your inheritance Mrs. Bradshaw. You need to come down to my office at 632 Pear Street. It's very important Mrs. Bradshaw. You need to come down as soon as possible," he stated with an urgent tone.

"Okay, I'll come down tomorrow, thank you," she said. "What's your name?"

"Oh I'm sorry ma'am. I'm Thomas Brooks, attorney at law," he answered quickly.

"Thank you," she uttered.

"You're welcome Mrs. Bradshaw. I'll see you tomorrow then," he told her.

As if she did not have, enough on her mind today, now she had one more thing to add to her dilemma. What could he want that was so important? What could he want from her? Yes, he said inheritance but he did not say where. She had no relatives around here. She was from Harrison, Arkansas. Did her husband have relatives around here? He told her that his people all lived in South Carolina. She went through all the papers in the house and there was not a clue about any of his people dying. She would just have to wait until tomorrow to see what he wanted. When Bryon and Amy got home from school, she told them about the strange phone call.

"What'd he want Mom?" Amy asked.

"I don't know I've got to go to his office tomorrow. He said something about inheritance," she told them.

"Inheritance? Who died?" Bryon asked.

"I don't know. It sounds like a big mystery to me," she told them.

"He should of told you," Bryon said.

"Let's watch a movie, I'll make popcorn," she suggested.

"Okay," Amy agreed. "Can we pick one?"

"Yes of course, pick something good," she said nodding.

While the movie played, she did not have her mind on watching. Her mind was on what the phone call involved. She hated mysteries and this started out like one without a doubt. Well regardless what it was she could always sell the place or the land. Could Bill be from some place that he never told her? William Bradshaw is whom she married, and he told her he grew up in a small town near Brownsville, South Carolina. Bill is what everyone called him. Losing a loved one takes a toll on anyone. She was not sure how she was going to cope with this for sure, but she had to try.

The next morning she made sure Bryon, Amy got off to school, and then she went uptown. She stopped at a café that she had not been in for a long time. Angie was surprised that Betty still worked here. She had not talked to her for a long time.

"Angie Bradshaw, I haven't seen you for a long time," Betty told her. "How you been?"

"I've been okay," she answered.

"I heard about Bill, I'm terribly sorry Angie," Betty said sincerely.

"I miss him," Angie uttered.

"I know you do Angie. A lot of people's gonna miss him. He was a good man," she said as she wiped her eyes.

Angie knew Betty since she was ten years old when her parents moved here from Arkansas. She never realized until now how long she lived here. She drank her coffee and then she left the café.

It was not just Betty, but many others around town acted as if they owed Bill a great debt of gratitude in some way. She walked two blocks to the attorney's office, and walked inside. She stopped at the front desk and waited for the woman to get off the phone. A minute later, she hung the phone up and looked up.

"May I help you?" she asked.

"I'm here to see Thomas Brooks," she told her.

"He won't be here until nine thirty. You can wait over there if you'd like," she said.

"Okay, thank you," Angie said.

She picked up a magazine and thumbed through the pages. Nothing held her attention so she picked up another magazine. Before she knew it, she heard the front door open and close.

"Good morning Mr. Brooks. There's a lady waiting to see you," she informed him.

A minute later, he walked to where she sat. He looked down at her with a slight frown. He had short cut brown hair, and was dressed in a gray business suit.

"Good morning," he said. "May I help you?"

"You called me yesterday," she reminded him.

"Oh yes, you must be Angie Bradshaw," she said as he smiled.

"Yes sir," she answered.

"Come back to my office," he said.

Angie followed him down the hall and into a room with a desk that had stacks of papers on top. He walked around behind the desk and flopped down in the chair.

"A lawyer from a dinky town I've never heard of called me a week ago. I received a letter at the time of your husband's death so I waited for a few days. Since your husband has passed on it now fall in your hands. In two weeks, there will be a reading of the will in Hagon's Bluff," he explained.

"Where's that at?" she asked.

"It's a small town in the mountains of West Virginia. The town has a population of about eight thousand people. I'm sorry to put you through this but the way I understand it you've inherited a healthy sum," he explained. "Can you make it there in time for the reading or will you need an extension?"

"Who am I supposed to see?" she inquired.

"Judge Russell ma'am," he answered.

"Write down how I'm supposed to get there. My kids will be out of school in a week and then we'll leave. It's a big mystery," she admitted. "How they related to me?"

"I have no idea, but it's imperative that you be there," he told her.

"Okay, get me some directions, and I'll leave in one week," she said unsure about leaving all of her friends and neighbors behind along with her two sisters.

"I'll do it, call me two days before you leave," he told her.

"Okay, but I don't understand," she insisted.

"You won't understand until you get there. Who knows what kind of challenge you'll face. I know I'd be leery about this sort of thing. You can read the letter if you want," he said handing her a single sheet of paper.

She sat and read the letter slowly. She skimmed through the heading past the business title into the first paragraph. I'm contacting you to inform you that William Bradshaw's uncle died three weeks ago. The only heir is Mr. Bradshaw, and he needs to come to Hagon's Bluff for the reading of the will at ten a. m. on June tenth. Please inform him to be there. It's very important that he appears," it read.

"That's basically what you've told me already," she told him. "This all that came?"

"Yes it is. I'm sorry I don't have more information for you," he said.

"That's fine, I'll figure it out as I go," she uttered getting up.

"I'm sure you will. It's not much to go on. I'm sorry but it don't answer any questions. You don't have much to look forward to except a big question mark. I do wish you the best of luck Mrs. Bradshaw," he told her.

"Thank you, I'd better go," she said walking toward the door.

She wanted to get away as soon as possible. She had a lot of thinking to do. She drove home to start getting ready to go to Hagon's Bluff wherever that was. Did she have enough money to make such a trip? Her husband took care of the bills so she really did not know what was in the bank.

When Bryon and Amy got home from school, she called them into the kitchen. In a way, she hated to tell them because they probably had plans for the summer. Well anyway, they should not be gone long just to be there for the reading of the will.

"I have something very important to tell you that might change our lives for ever. I don't know this for sure, but we have to go on a trip as soon as school's out for the summer. Your father and I inherited something important. We've got to make a trip to Hagon's Bluff for the reading of the will on June tenth. I don't know what we'll inherit for sure," she told them.

"You're not making any sense Mom," Bryon stated.

"You're not coming to the point Mom," Amy said.

"I don't know what the point is Amy. All I know is Judge Russell sent a letter to Thomas Brooks here in town for us to go to Hagon's Bluff," she told them. "Wouldn't you rather know what we're to inherit than to lose it all?"

"Well yeah I guess so," Bryon said skeptically.

"I'd like to know Mom," Amy quickly told her.

"All right, it's settled then. When you get out of school Friday afternoon, I'll pick you up. I'll have our suitcases in the car and we'll leave then," she explained.

"Sure Mom," Bryon said shrugging his shoulders.

"I'm ready now Mom," Amy stated.

"You need to pick out clothes for two weeks. Pack them neatly in suitcases. I only hope it'll be worth while. We could inherit a big house and a lot of land," she said wishfully.

"Where's this place at?" Bryon asked.

"It's in the mountains of West Virginia. That's all I know right now," she told them.

After supper, they sat down to watch television. Angie had a feeling that this was going to be a long week. She had a feeling that she could not explain but it kept nagging at her mind. Something did not fit perfectly for some reason. She had a feeling that it was about her deceased husband. What brought all of these things about? Where did it come from?

Writers have written about how people act when faced with a challenge. Most people felt comfortable in a rut where it felt safe and secure. Her husband died with a calamity of the worst kind. What she loved and cherished the most cancer took away from her leaving her with loved filled memories.

2

Friday afternoon Angie parked her car in the school parking lot and waited for the school bell. She had all of their suitcases packed in the car ready to go on their trip. Angie's sister Helen, promised to watch over her house while she was gone. Angie grew impatient waiting for school to get out. What were they going to get into was constantly on her mind. At times, she could not stand it any longer and she had to force herself to think about something else.

Soon she could see Bryon and Amy walking toward the car. Angie was ready to get this over with as soon as possible. She started the car and drove out of town. When it started to get dark, she found a motel and a place to eat. They were in the mountains of North Carolina. At a nearby café, they sat down to eat. The children were tired of riding. Some of the people that came in looked at them oddly. Yes, they were strangers. They sat down in a booth where they would be comfortable.

"May I help you?" a young woman asked.

"Yes, when I came in the door I saw you had meatloaf for a special. I'll take one of them, and the children want cheeseburgers and fries. Pepsi for them and I'll have coffee," she told her.

"Yes ma'am, I'll bring your drinks out right away," she said.

Only six people were in the café. There were two elderly couples, and two middle-aged men sat at the counter. A few minutes later, the waitress brought their drinks. Twenty minutes later, she brought their food to the table.

Five hours after they ate breakfast they rode across the Virginia state line. If she read the map correctly, they would be in West Virginia soon. When they rode into West Virginia, she stopped at a gas station to ask directions. She parked the car and went inside.

"Could you tell me how to get to Hagon's Bluff?" she inquired.

"What you wanna go there for?" the attendant asked.

"That ain't a good place to go," another man said.

"Why not?" Angie asked.

"There be strange things going on there," he answered.

Angie was not going to be intimidated. She was determined to go regardless. Maybe those two men were trying to scare her. What could be so scary about a town?

"It's sixty-two miles from here. You gotta watch closely for the little sign. Then you've got twenty miles of gravel roads," a third man told her.

"Thank you so much gentlemen," she said.

"Yes ma'am, you're welcome," he told her.

She walked out the door upset and got in the car. In a way, she felt disgusted because of the way they talked to her.

"We've got about eighty-five miles to go. We've got to find a place to stay and go up there on the tenth early that morning," she said.

"What if there's no where to stay when we get there?" Amy asked.

"I'm sure the late Mr. Bradshaw lived in a house," she mentioned.

"Shouldn't we wait until the will is read?" Bryon asked.

"Yes, we don't have a choice," Angie, said.

"That's only a few days away," Amy committed.

"What was Mr. Bradshaw like?" Bryon asked.

"I've got no idea. Your father's parents is the only ones I've met. His parents acted nice, but as soon as we were married, they left. At the time, I thought it was a little strange," she explained.

"I wonder why they never stayed?" Amy asked.

"Who knows," she remarked.

Suddenly she slammed on the brakes barely missing a small deer. After a minute, she started the car moving again. The trees were close to the road, anything could jump out in their path, and get ran over. Big rocks rested among the trees with moss growing on top.

Four hours later, they rode past a little sign pointing the way to Hagon's Bluff. Ten miles down the road, they came to a town down in a big valley. She stopped at a motel and went inside to register.

"May I help you ma'am?" a middle-aged woman asked.

"Yes, I'd like a room for three nights," she answered.

The woman wore her gray-streaked brown hair up in an old-fashioned bun. Around her neck was a gold chain attached to a pair of reading glasses. She wore a loose fitting floral print dress with slippers on her feet.

"We've got a room with two beds," she told her. "Will that be okay?"

"Yes, that'll be fine," Angie, agreed.

"That'll be twenty-five dollars per night. You have room 106," she told her.

"Is there a café nearby?" Angie asked.

"There's a place two blocks down the street on your left. It's not fancy but they got good food," she answered.

"Thank you so much," Angie said picking up the key.

"I hope you enjoy your stay," she remarked.

She walked outside and drove the car slowly until she found the room. Then they carried their bags in the room. They left the car in front of the room and walked to the café. A young woman waited on them that liked to talk. This time of day there was not many customers to wait on.

"What county is this?" Angie asked.

"It's Roosevelt County ma'am," she answered.

"Is Hagon's Bluff in this county?" Angie inquired.

"Yes ma'am," she answered.

"You know Judge Russell? He here in town?" she asked.

"Not personally ma'am, but he'd be up at the courthouse," she answered.

"That's good," Angie, uttered.

"You in trouble?" she asked.

"Oh no, it's nothing like that," Angie assured her. "You know anything about Hagon's Bluff?"

"It's a small town. There's a grocery store, a gas station, and that's about all I remember," she explained.

"Okay, thank you so much," she said.

After they finished eating, they walked back to the room. They took showers and got ready for bed. The television did not work very well and they gave up trying to watch anything.

The next morning they went to eat at the café. This time there was a woman in her mid-fifties that waited on them. Bryon and Amy were not very hungry this morning.

After asking four people at the courthouse, they finally found the right place to go. The old courthouse had hardwood floors that squeaked as they walked down the hall. They walked into a small office at the end of the hallway. Inside sat a middle-aged secretary sitting behind a desk. There were many file cabinets along the wall behind her.

"May I help you?" the woman asked.

"We just came into town yesterday, and I'd like to see Judge Russell for five minutes. My name's Angie Bradshaw and my husband was William. We came for the reading of Mr. Bradshaw's will," she explained.

"Wait here," she said getting up.

She opened a door and walked into another room. A few minutes later, she returned with a man following her.

"I'm so glad you came Mrs. Bradshaw. William Bradshaw inherited the property," he told her. "You know where he's at?"

"My husband passed away five weeks ago," she answered.

"I'm so sorry ma'am, I had no idea," he said shaking his head.

"He'd been very sick for the past year. We knew it was coming for a while. The way I understand it this falls in my lap now," she told him. "Am I right?"

"Yes ma'am that's right," he said nodding his head. "What you planning to do with the property?"

"I don't know what the will says, I'm totally in the dark," she told him. "Will the reading of the will take place here or in Hagon's Bluff?"

"It'll be day after tomorrow at Hagon's Bluff. There's a community hall next to the magistrates office. That's where Robert Lansing will read the will. He was Morgan Bradshaw's lawyer in all legal matters," he told her.

"That's good, I was wondering who the lawyer was over the estate. Now I have an idea what's going to take place in two days," she said nodding her head.

"It's a big responsibility to say the least ma'am. Robert Lansing will help you if you need some legal help. There'll be a lot of things to change into your name, and that will take several hundred dollars," he told her.

Bryon and Amy sat listening not believing their ears. They did not know what they were going to have yet. If they were going to have a place maybe she could have a horse. Amy loved horses, and she wanted to own a horse.

"We'll see you later then," he said.

"Thank you so much for your help," Angie told him.

"You're welcome ma'am. I've got to get back to work," he said.

"Let's go kids," Angie said.

When they left the office, Angie wanted to go to the library. She was curious about Morgan Bradshaw. They spent part of the morning at the courthouse. She made copies of deeds and later birth and death certificates. She made copies of any newspaper articles that she could find.

On June tenth, they left the motel early, ate, and then she drove to Hagon's Bluff. Angie parked the car next to the magistrate's office and they got out looking around. Then she spotted a store down the street a hundred yards. The door to the community hall was locked shut. They had some time to kill so they walked to the store. It was an old store made of cement blocks with old hardwood floors. There were several racks made of wood that held food items.

"Good morning," a slim middle-aged woman said.

"Good morning," Angie said cheerfully.

"You gonna stay long in town?" she inquired.

"I don't know, I've got a lot of things to do," she answered.

"What do you mean?" she asked.

"A lot of paperwork," she answered. "Do you own this store?"

"No ma'am, I lease it from Morgan Bradshaw. Now that he's passed on I don't know what'll happen," she said shaking her head.

"I'll come back later to talk to you. We're just killing time right now," Angie told her. "You going to the reading of the will?"

"What time is it?" she asked.

"Ten o'clock this morning," she answered.

"That's half an hour from now," she stated.

"Yes I know, we'll see you later," Angie, said.

They left the store and walked back to the meeting hall. She had a feeling that there was going to be some upset people. She did not want to do anything until she talked to the lawyer. The front door was unlocked and standing open. When they walked inside a man in a black suit was standing at the end of a bench looking for papers in a briefcase. The community hall was one long room with no partitions. There was several benches and chairs in rows.

"Aw, good morning," he said.

"Good morning," Angie replied.

"I'm Robert Lansing," he said. "And you are?"

"Angie Bradshaw," she answered.

"Where's William Bradshaw?" he asked.

"He passed away five weeks ago," she answered.

"I'm so sorry ma'am," he said looking at the floor a moment.

"He had cancer for the last two years, and it finally over took him," she explained.

"So's everything's in your lap now," he mentioned.

"Yes sir," she agreed.

"I'm here to help you if you want," he suggested.

"From the way Judge Russell talked I'll be needing a lot of help," she said.

"Most of the things that need changed are formalities. Here comes Judge Russell finally, it's almost ten o'clock," he said looking up.

Angie turned to look at the door as he came inside. He was carrying a briefcase.

Bryon and Amy were walking around the hall looking for something of interest. They were bored to death this morning.

"Everyone here?" Judge Russell asked.

A pot-bellied man in a brown business suit stood to address the judge and lawyer. He took the lead for the rest of the people here. He was clean-shaven and bald on top.

"Some of the others are supposed to come but I don't know if they'll make a showing or not," he said.

"Thank you Mayor Brown," Judge Russell said. "What about Morgan Bradshaw's children?"

"I don't know your honor," he answered.

"We'll wait ten minutes and then proceed as planned. Everyone was sent a notice to appear," he stated.

"Would everyone come up front please?" Robert Lansing asked. "I don't want to lose my voice talking loud."

When everyone sat down he held up a stack of papers stapled together and stood in the center of the room. Then he looked out over the room for a moment for newcomers.

"I Morgan Bradshaw, being of sound mind and body leave my holdings to the following. To my three children I leave all of my property in Tabor's Point to be divided equally. They can do as fitting for them. My six businesses in Hagon's Bluff, house and forty acres, and the two hundred and fifty acres in the hills I leave to William Bradshaw. All of the land in Hagon's Bluff I leave to William Bradshaw," Robert read slowly. "Does everyone understand this?"

All of their heads nodded up and down several times. Not one person objected verbally. Getting any one of them to talk openly was a task.

"Since William Bradshaw passed away recently he inheritance will go to his wife and family," he added.

"That's not fair," a man hollered out.

"It would be the same if William died at a later date," he told them. "What's the difference? There any more questions now?"

No one uttered a sound for a minute or longer. No one disagreed with Robert so that meant he was finished. Angie kept her eyes forward listening to Robert.

"Here's a copy of the will Mrs. Bradshaw, the keys to the house, and a list of the renters. It's all yours now Mrs. Bradshaw," he explained.

Her heart sunk a little as he place all of this in her arms. An overbearing responsibility rested on her shoulders now. She had so much to do to get everything straightened out.

3

They walked out to the car and Angie drove to the house where Morgan Bradshaw lived. She turned onto a gravel lane that led to a white two-story house surrounded by trees and shrubs. On the west, side of the house was a two-car garage. She could not look inside because of the tightly shut doors. Angie parked the car in front of the garage and they got out. She tried each key in the back door lock, and the fourth key unlocked the door. The door opened into a big kitchen that was fairly clean but smelled of stale air. Along the outside wall was a long counter with a double sink under the window looking out into the back yard. A small kitchen table with four chairs sat in the middle of the room. Above the counter were tall cupboards that reached to the ceiling.

"Well, what do you think?" Angie asked.

"It's not what I expected," Amy uttered.

"What did you expect," she asked.

"Something like a cottage," Amy remarked.

"Let's find out what the rest of the house looks like," Angie suggested.

The living room looked cozy with a fireplace and several stuffed chairs scattered around the room. Downstairs was one bedroom, a washroom, and a study. Upstairs were four bedrooms each painted white. Angie went back downstairs to look around in the bedroom for important papers.

That afternoon they went to town to get supplies to clean the house. Amy was excited about having her own room. Bryon's room was the last down the hall. It had a window that looked out into the back yard. Bryon was more interested about what was in the hills. Exploring was something that he loved to do.

That evening after supper, Angie sat down in the living room to relax. All of a sudden, she screamed when she saw the figure of a man looking in the window. By the time, she got up, opened the door, and looked outside there was no one there. The thought of someone watching them was very revolting. A few minutes later, she sat down again. She was tired; they cleaned the entire kitchen, the hallway, and made up three beds for them to sleep in tonight.

The next morning while she was cooking breakfast she saw a boy and girl looking in the kitchen window. They stood and watched them as if this was an every day thing to do. Angie waved to them, and then she motioned for them to come inside. They appeared to be about twelve or thirteen years of age. Why did they just stand there?

"Go see if they'll come inside Bryon," she suggested.

"Okay Mom," he said nodding his head.

He went outside to try to coax them inside. Talking to them did not do any good. They just ignored him as they stood stubbornly still. Then Bryon took the girls hand and tried to take her inside. If she came inside would he follow? The boy shoved Bryon hard backwards causing him to stumble and fall on the ground. Bryon disgustedly got up, brushed himself off, and walked into the house.

"I tried Mom, but they're so stubborn," he told her.

"Yes I know, I watched you," she said.

"What kind of people is that?" Amy asked.

"I don't know honey, they're just kids. I think there's something wrong with their lives," Angie told her.

Angie cooked the children an egg apiece, put two slices of bacon on top and put it between two slices of bread. Then she walked outside with the sandwiches and slowly handed the sandwiches to the two children. They held the sandwiches in their hands and continued to look in the window. Disgustedly, she walked back onto the back porch and then she peaked around the corner of the door. They stood wolfing the sandwiches down as fast as they could swallow. They acted as if they had not had anything to eat for a week or more.

Then she walked in the house to find Bryon and Amy watching the children outside. They had never see anyone act that way before. The two children acted very strange beyond what Bryon and Amy knew was reality.

"Who are they?" Amy asked.

"I don't know," Angie, answered.

"Their mind ain't right Mom," Bryon stated.

"Isn't right Bryon," Angie corrected him.

"Regardless Mom, they're lacking something big," he stated.

"It may take a few days for them to come around. I'd like to know where they live," she told them.

"Who knows," Amy uttered.

The next time they looked out the window, the children were gone. She looked around the back yard and she could not see them anywhere. After breakfast, they walked outside to check out the barn. Angie hoped that those children did not live in a place like the barn.

They had to push hard to get one of the doors to roll on the rusty track above. The barn remained closed up for a long time. In the center of the barn sat what appeared to be three cars each covered up with a heavy canvas. Angie picked up the corner of the canvas and underneath was a fender of a dark blue car. She could not tell what kind car it was for sure.

"Help me lift this Bryon," she told him.

"What is it Mom?" he asked.

"It's a car of some kind," she answered.

They lifted the canvas so it exposed one side of the car. Then they let the canvas back down and went to the next. A spring buggy sat in the far corner of the barn covered with a thick layer of dust. As they looked around the barn, they found many old tools, harness, oil lamps, and several other things.

"What's up there?" Bryon asked.

"I don't know," she answered.

"Let's find out," Bryon suggested.

"Okay, but you stay down here," she said firmly.

"Come on Mom," he uttered.

In the corner stood a ladder that the carpenter nailed to the wall so it would be out of the way when they put hay in the loft. She slowly climbed the ladder and soon she was in the loft. There had not been any hay put up here for years. In the back corner of the loft, there were several empty wood boxes stacked up in a pile. There did not appear to be anything of value in the boxes she walked back to the ladder. When she got down the ladder, they locked the doors on the barn and walked back to the house. The garage was the next place she wanted to check out.

She searched the key ring for a key that would fit the garage door, and none would fit. Then she went in the house to search for another key ring. An hour later, she found a ring of keys and one of the keys unlocked the door. Inside was an old Ford pickup, a workbench, and several tools that hung on a pegboard or cluttered around in a red toolbox. Then she went back to the house to search for car titles.

With a handful of papers, she went to the lawyer's office in Tabor's Point. When she walked into his office, he looked frustrated for some reason.

"Here's all the paperwork I can find easily. I'd like the title to the Ford pickup changed over first. I need it to haul trash off to the dump," she told him.

"Okay, let me look through all of this. Go over to the courthouse to get copies of all the property he owned," he suggested.

"Okay, I'll be back," she said.

She got copies, and went back to his office. Then they went home, to start cleaning again.

The next morning while Angie was cooking breakfast she noticed that the boy and girl were standing in the same spot looking in the window. She went outside and tried to get them to come in the house. They would not budge. Then Angie thought that she get them to come in the house. They would not budge. Then Angie thought that she would try something else.

"Get in the house," she hollered loudly.

They jumped as if they were coming out of a trance or something. They turned and walked into the house, and stood near the table looking at the floor. She was very surprised that they did what she told them. What kind of life did these kids have? Now if she could only get them to talk to her.

"What's your names?" Angie asked.

They stood looking at the floor as they stood near the table. She could not figure out why they were acting this way. She had not done anything to them; she only wanted to help them. She hoped that they would open up soon.

"My name's Bryon."

"My name's Amy."

Both of them looked up for a flicker of a second. That was the only reaction that they showed that someone was talking to them. They were scared to death with the thought of what the woman might do to them this morning for looking in the window. Their mother would have beaten then for acting this way. They used to look in the window every morning when Mr. Bradshaw lived here and he ignored them all the time. They stood many mornings very hungry and he acted as if they were part of the window. What would they do if this woman beat them?

Soon Angie had breakfast cooked and they sat down to eat. The two children still stood between the table and the door. Angie got back up and motioned for them to sit down. They still stood like statues.

"Move!" she exclaimed.

They quickly moved to two empty chairs and sat down. Why did they only move when she hollered at them? Angie said the blessing over the food and then they began to eat. Surprisingly they used a spoon to get the grits in their mouth and swallowed it straight down. They used their fingers to eat the rest of the food.

After everyone ate breakfast, Angie and Amy washed and dried the dishes. When they put the dishes away, Angie sat down next to the girl.

"What's your name?" Angie asked softly. "There's nothing to be afraid of."

"You'll kick up out of the house," the girl said.

"No I won't," Angie, told her.

"Will too," she retorted.

"I've got no reason to do that," she said firmly. "Your parents kicked you out of the house?"

Both of them nodded their heads several times. This was very sad for her to watch. Both of them looked very scared as they looked at her. How could such things happen to children in this modern day and age?

"Momma will beat us if we don't leave. She's got a man caller that comes to see her in the mornings," the girl said quickly.

"What's your name?" Angie asked again.

"I Jenny, he Jason. He can't talk good," she answered.

She slobbered a little in the corners of her mouth as she talked. Both of them had blonde hair and hazel eyes. They had slender faces, but the boy was bigger.

"How old are you?" Angie asked.

"We're almost thirteen," she answered.

"You're twins ain't you?" she inquired.

"What's that?" Jenny asked.

"Was you born on the same day?" she asked.

"I don't know," she uttered.

"Twins are born on the same day minutes apart," she said. "Why do you look in the window?"

"You new; Mr. Bradshaw never paid us no mind," she answered.

"Why are you beaten?" Angie inquired.

"I don't know," she uttered.

Jason pulled up the back of her shirt and on her back was several black and blue welts about two inches wide. Then she pulled up Jason's shirt and there were many welts on his back. It was plain to see that someone beat them repeatedly with a belt.

Angie felt a chill go up her back as she listened to them talk. How anyone could treat her children like that was beyond her. Angie had never faced anything like this before.

"Beat us," Jason said with a strained slurred voice.

"I'm so sorry," Angie, told them.

Jenny never knew what it was like to live the life of a girl. She wore boy's clothes, and her mother cut her hair as short as Jason's did. If a person did not look closely, they would have thought that they were looking at two boys. That was societies viewpoint.

An hour after Jenny and Jason ate they got up and walked out the door without saying anything. They watched them in total surprise.

"Where they going Mom?" Amy asked.

"I don't know," she answered.

"Did you see where they'd been beat Mom?" Bryon asked.

"Yes, that's uncalled for," she said shaking her head.

"What we gonna do with all this stuff Mom?" he asked.

"Sell it or give it away, we need to get this place cleaned up," she told them.

"Yeah, but where do we start?" he inquired.

"In the front room," she stated.

They set to work cleaning out old newspapers, old magazines, and old mail that was not any good. Each piece of mail she had to go through checking the contents. It looked as if he had not thrown anything away in the last ten years. They worked into the afternoon when she realized that she had to call the power company and the telephone office.

4

The next morning they went to Tabor's Point. She wanted to take the paper work that they found to the lawyer's office. Today was a bright sunny day filled with expectations.

"Good morning," Robert said as they came in his office.

"Good morning," she told him. "You find out anything?"

"Four of the six businesses want to buy if they can come to agreeable terms. As far as the pickup, you can go get tags for it. State Farm has the lowest rates here in town," he explained.

"That's good, now all I have to do is learn how to drive it," she uttered. "What about the people that want to buy?" Who handles that paperwork?"

"You do need a legal agreement that's binding. You've got to discuss the price with them," he suggested.

"Okay, thank you," she said.

It took over an hour at the DMV office to get tags for the pickup. Now she would have to get it inspected. On the way home, she asked if there was a mechanic in Hagon's Bluff. She found his shop a block north of Main Street. It was a cement block building with two big bay doors with a half dozen cars parked in front. When she got out of the car, a middle-aged man came outside wiping his hands on a grease rag.

"May I help you?" he asked.

"Yes sir," she answered. "Could you come up to the house and get my pickup running?"

"Where you live?" he asked.

"At Morgan Bradshaw's old house, I'm Angie Bradshaw," she informed him.

"Give me about a hour and I'll be up," he said.

"Okay thank you," she told him.

Then she drove home to wait on him. She still had piles of papers to go through. Later, they could hear a truck coming up the gravel lane. It had to be the mechanic. She walked out to the garage to unlock the door. He came walking up to her carrying a small toolbox in his hand.

"I'm so glad you came," she said.

"You're lucky I'm here at all," he uttered.

"Why's that?" she inquired.

"I vowed I'd never come back to this place again. Three times, I worked on a car and old Morgan said it didn't run good afterwards. He never paid me for the work. I reckon I can't be that way now that the old coot passed on. He was an ornery cuss at times," he told her. "You inherit this place?"

"Yes sir, it went to my husband but he passed away recently," she told him.

"I'm so sorry ma'am, I had no right to pry," he uttered.

"It's okay sir. We're trying to get this mess straightened out," she told him.

"I'm Ben Jenkins," he said.

"My name's Angie Bradshaw. It's so good to meet you sir," she said.

"You say it's in the garage?" he asked.

"Yes sir," she answered.

She led the way through the walk in door into the garage. She had tried to lift the door earlier but it wouldn't budge. He sat his toolbox down on the bench.

"Oh yes, I remember this truck. I put an engine in it two years ago. He paid me for that job," he told her.

"Here's the keys for the pickup. I can't get the door to open, it won't budge," she said.

He was about forty years old she judged. He had brown hair, brown eyes, and a slightly rounded face. He was clean-shaven with short side burns, and acted very knowledgeable about cars.

"It's a sixty nine Ford. It had a three sixty engine in it and I put in a three ninety engine. I doubt if he put on two hundred miles since I put the engine in. His health got so bad that he couldn't push the clutch pedal down," he explained.

"I hope you don't mind me asking questions do you?" she inquired.

"No ma'am, go right ahead," he answered.

He lifted the hood and checked over the engine. He cleaned the battery cables, checked the oil level, checked the water in the radiator, and checked the air cleaner. Then he walked around and got in behind the steering wheel. He pumped the accelerator pedal several times and turned the key switch to the start position. On the second try, the engine came to life. He got out leaving the engine run at an idle and looked around on the bench for a pry bar. He found a crowbar and used it to pry the door up that was stuck on the bottom. After the first two inches, the door rolled up easily.

"Get in ma'am," he told her.

Angie walked around and got in the passenger side. Bryon and Amy stood watching as he backed the pickup out of the garage. She could count the times on one hand that she rode in a pickup with a standard transmission. He drove down to the highway and turned the pickup around. Then he got out the door, walked around to the other side, and got in. He coached her on how to drive a pickup with a standard transmission. Angie killed the engine twice before she could manage the clutch. She picked up the driving skills faster than she thought she would, and shifted gears. She pulled up in front of the garage and shut the engine off. Then she got out and walked to the open door.

"That wasn't too hard," she uttered. "Where can I get it inspected?"

"I can inspect it ma'am," he told her.

"That's good, I was hoping I wouldn't have to drive it to Tabor's Point," she told him.

They stood in front of the garage talking. She did not know much about this area. She had so many questions to ask.

"You know anything about the cars in the barn?" she asked.

"I know about one car," he answered.

"You know anything about a boy and a girl about twelve years old that live around here?" she inquired. "Their names are Jenny and Jason."

"Now you want me to get in a pickle. I reckon I can," he said.

"Where do they live?" she asked.

"Up in the hills yonder. If I remember right their parents leased their land from Morgan," he told her.

"How far away?" she asked.

"About a mile from here," he answered.

"What's their parents like?" she inquired.

"He works construction jobs. He's out of town a lot. She lays up a lot. That's all I'm going to say about the matter," he said curtly.

"Would you look at the cars in the barn please?" she asked.

"Yeah sure," he answered.

"When would you have time to service the truck?" she asked.

"Tomorrow would be fine. Bring it down to the shop," he suggested.

They walked out to the barn and he looked at the cars. When he finished they walked back to the garage. What he saw impressed him.

"When would you have time to check them out?" she inquired.

"Later in the summer ma'am, I think. I can find a buyer for one of the cars I believe," he told her.

"Okay, thank you so much," she said. "Where does everyone haul trash off to?"

"I'd burn the paper and the rest I'd haul off. Just as you're leaving town there's a road to the left. It's up there a couple of miles," he explained.

"Okay, thank you, I'll see you tomorrow," she said.

"Yes ma'am, I'd better get back to work," he told her.

That afternoon she went to talk to the store renters. She went to the grocery store first. She was not sure where the other places were at for sure.

"May I help you," the woman behind the counter asked.

"Yes ma'am, I came to talk to you about this place. Mr. Lansing said you wanted to buy," she answered.

"Yes we do if the payments ain't too high," she answered surprised.

"We've got to get the place appraised so we've got a guide line to work from. I want to be fair about this," Angie told her.

"We'd rather pay you than pay all that interest to the bank," she suggested.

"Yes we can do that. We can work the details out with the lawyer. A simple contract is all we need," she told her.

"You're a lot easier to deal with than Morgan Bradshaw," she stated.

"I really don't want to deal with a bunch of details. If you want to buy, you can do that. My lawyer can draw up a contract for us," she told her politely. "You know anything about Jenny and Jason? Do they go to school?"

"I'm sure you know what their mother does by now. No, they don't go to school that I know of. That's the Thompkins family. Ralph Thompkins is gone most of the time. When he's at home, he drinks a lot. "It's a sad state of affairs," she explained.

"For the children it's sad," Angie said. "What's your name?

"It's Hazel, my husband Bradford McCormick and I run this place," she answered.

"I wanted to know about the kids. They stand outside my window and look inside," she mentioned.

"They did that when Morgan lived there," she said.

"Thank you so much, I'll talk to you later," Angie told her.

"Okay," she said nodding her head.

A week later, Jenny and Jason came to the house and stood looking in the window for the fourth time. Angie went outside to try to get them to come inside the house.

"Move," Angie said loudly.

They quickly turned and walked into the house. They sat down at the table but they would not put their backs against the chair. When Amy went to the cupboard to get extra plates she saw blood on the back of Jenny's blouse. Amy whispered in her mother's ear about what she saw. Angie decided to wait until they finished eating before she looked at Jenny's back.

After they washed the dishes and dried them, they put them away. Then Angie took Jenny to the bathroom. She unbuttoned her blouse and looked at her back. There were fresh welts on her back and in two places close together, the skin was broke letting blood ooze out. She had trouble cleaning the wounds as tears ran down her cheeks. How in the world could anyone treat a child like this was far beyond her reasoning. She washed the wounds good with peroxide and then she put a gauze bandage over the wound.

At first, Jenny was very scared. Jenny's nerves calmed down when she found out that Angie was not going to hurt her. Angie's fingers had a tender touch to them as she worked on her back. Angie was nice and she wanted to take care of her.

"If you come for breakfast tomorrow please knock on the door," Angie suggested. "Would you do that for me?"

"Yes ma'am," she answered.

She went into the kitchen and brought Jason to the bathroom. She took off his shirt and looked at his back. His skin was not broke or cut but his skin showed bruises dark in color. The tender places she washed with peroxide on a cotton ball. Then she had him put his shirt back on.

"Okay Jason," she said.

Angie had to go to town the next day to talk to the store renters. In the middle of the afternoon, she stopped at the grocery store again. She was talking to Hazel when a blonde-headed woman came in the door. While she was looking for items to buy, she kept watching Hazel and Angie. Several minutes later, the woman sat several items down on the counter.

"Hurry up now, I don't wanna be late," she said sarcastically.

"Yes ma'am," Hazel said.

She checked the items off as quickly as possible. She told her the amount and collected the money. Then she bagged her purchases. While Hazel was busy, doing that the woman looked Angie up and down.

Who you supposed to be?" she asked with a touch of hatefulness.

"That's no way to talk to someone Maggie," Hazel said sternly.

"I'll talk the way I want, she don't belong here. She's not welcome here," she said with venom.

"I'm so sorry," Angie said.

Maggie glared at her as she picked up her bags and stomped toward the door. Angie had a feeling she would meet people like her here.

"Who was that?" Angie asked.

"Maggie Thompkins, you're her landlord," she answered.

"Where does she live?" she inquired.

"Up in the hills, they live the closest to town," she said.

"Who's mother is Jenny and Jason's," Angie asked.

"Maggie Thompkins," she answered. "You know those two?"

"Yes, they've had breakfast with me more than once," Angie, replied. "Why does their father beat them?"

"It's not him, it's her. That's why those two are like that because of her. That's what drugs will get ya," she explained.

"Drugs?" Angie asked surprised.

"Yeah, she took cocaine, crack, and I don't know what all when she was pregnant with them. Whatever's in the mother will be in the children when they're born. Now days all she takes is pills because she don't have the money for the hard stuff," she explained.

"They told me they have to leave the house in the mornings because their mother's got a male caller," Angie mentioned.

"Yeah everyone knows about them. Don't rock the boat too hard," she said.

"What you mean?" Angie inquired.

"Regardless, they're still her kids," she answered.

"You'd rock the boat if you saw their backs," she stated.

"Their backs?" Hazel asked surprised.

"Where they've been beaten," Angie said sternly.

"Oh no, I didn't realize that. A child needs to be beaten on the bottom and no where else," she stated.

"I feel sorry for them. They don't need to be treated that way, they're not animals," she told her.

"Oh no, something ought to be done about that," Hazel uttered.

"I agree, but I can't take on the whole community by myself," Angie stated.

"I'll help you as much as I can," Hazel mentioned.

"I appreciate your support," she uttered.

"Glad to help," she told her.

"I'd better go," she said.

"Okay, keep me posted," Hazel told her.

"You know everyone around here?" Angie inquired.

"Yeah, I reckon," she answered.

"How many people live here in town?" she asked.

"About eight thousand might be more now," she answered.

"What was Morgan Bradshaw like? What happened to his wife?" she inquired.

"His wife died of cancer years ago. He was okay for an old coot. He died of cancer you know. He was a good man but he had his ways. I thought some of his ways was obnoxious. He was fair but harsh," she explained.

"My husband died of cancer. We had his funeral two weeks before we came up here. The kids got out of school first," Angie, told her.

"I'm sorry to hear that," Hazel uttered.

"I'll talk to you later," she said.

"Okay, have a good day," Hazel told her.

5

Tomorrow Angie wanted to go see the lawyer. She wanted to know what she could do and what she could not. Those two children were on her mind a lot. She thought that she would like to take care of them. They needed someone that would take time with them, and take care of them. Did their mother love and take care of them?

Why on Earth would she want to take care of two children like that? Maybe it was her calling. For Angie, it was heartbreaking to see welts up and down their backs.

Yesterday she sold the third business. Two of them were to make payments to Angie, and the third went through the bank. Hazel and her husband were the first to buy.

The next morning Jenny and Jason came to the house before Angie started breakfast. Jenny knocked on the door and Bryon let them inside. Jenny was crying and Jason was very upset.

"What's the matter?" Bryon asked.

They stood silently near the table wringing their hands. Jenny had been crying for a while, and Jason looked as if he wanted to cry. Angie held both of them in her arms a minute until they settled down. Jenny's crying slowed down with a few heart wrenching sobs. Angie stood crying as she held them tightly. Wherever she tried to put her hand on their backs, they would wince and pulled away. Then she released them and took Jenny by the hand to the bathroom. She took all of Jenny's clothes off. Jenny's back, buttocks, and the back of her legs had new welts over the top of old ones. On her back were three small cuts about an inch long each.

"We're going to put your clothes back on Jenny," Angie said as tears rolled down her cheeks.

"Okay," she agreed.

Jenny had stopped crying but she was still upset and she hurt all over. Angie helped her with her clothes.

"I want you to come with me Jenny. I'm taking you and your brother to the doctor," she told her. "Okay?"

"Yes ma'am," she answered.

"Let's go now," she told her.

Angie walked back to the kitchen to get the others. They were still sitting at the table.

"We're going to town right now. Hurry up," she said nervously.

Angie took Jason by the arm and led him outside with Jenny following along behind. Angie was glad that he was going willingly. She did not want to argue with him. They got in the car and she drove to Tabor's Point.

"Where we going Mom?" Amy asked.

"I'm taking Jenny and Jason to the doctor. Their backs could get infected," she answered.

Angie drove straight to the lawyer's office. She hoped that he would be there. This was something that could not wait.

"Good morning," the secretary said.

"Good morning," Angie replied. "Is Robert in?"

"Yes ma'am, let me get him," she said.

She got up and walked back to his office. Angie's mind was racing with what to do. A minute later, she came back to where Angie stood waiting.

"You can go on back Mrs. Bradshaw," she told her.

"Thank you," she said.

She walked down the hallway holding onto Jenny and Jason. She stopped in front of Robert holding onto them. She did not know how this was going to turn out but she had to try.

"Good morning," Robert said.

"Good morning, I need something done in a hurry. These two children can't keep on living the way they are. I would like custody of them. I need to take them to the doctor, but I need some legal help first. I know what can happen. They've been to the house several times, and each time they'd have fresh welts from being beaten. Their names is Jenny and Jason Thompkins. I need some help bad Robert," she said pleading almost in tears.

She turned them around and lifted their shirt a few inches for him to see their backs. He saw one of the cuts on Jenny's back and shook his head in shock.

"Just a minute, I'll get some help," Robert said.

He picked up the phone and called the sheriff's office. He kept looking at the children as if he was going into shock or something.

"Yes ma'am," he answered the phone. "Burt Johnson there?"

"He's not here," she told him.

"Where's he at?" he asked. "My name's Robert Lansing."

"At home," she answered.

"Call him and tell him to come to my office as soon as possible. This is an emergency ma'am," he said hanging up. "Who beat you?"

"Momma," Jenny answered.

"Hopefully he'll get here soon and we'll get this sorted out for you," he told her.

"Okay," Angie uttered.

Twenty minutes later, a tall man dressed in a sheriff's uniform came into the office. He wore a ball cap, and he had a slim face with a bushy mustache. By now, Jenny stopped crying but she clung tightly to Angie.

"What's the trouble Robert?" he asked.

"This is Angie Bradshaw. She inherited Morgan Bradshaw's place. These two children been coming to her house in the mornings and she's fed them. The other morning she saw blood on the back of the girl's shirt. They've been beaten severely from their shoulders to their knees. Mrs. Bradshaw wants temporary custody of these children because they don't need to be in the environment they're in. She came to see what legal course she could take," Robert explained.

"What's your names?" Burt asked.

"I Jenny, he Jason," she told him.

"He talk?" Burt asked.

"Very little, it's very hard for him," Angie told him.

"I reckon the best thing for us to do is go before Judge Russell," Burt stated. "You want to stay with Mrs. Bradshaw?"

Both of their heads bobbed up and down as they looked up at him. Jenny held Angie's arm tightly afraid to let go.

"Yes sir," Jenny said very nervously.

"Let's go now before he gets busy doing something else," Robert suggested.

"Call over there and see when we can see him," Burt said.

"Okay," he agreed.

"You can take them to the doctor Mrs. Bradshaw. Make sure you tell them you've already talked to me. My name's Burt Johnson ma'am. I'm sure they'll want to call the law on you," he explained.

"Okay, thank you so much sheriff," she said overjoyed.

Angie left the office with Jenny and Jason. Up front, she found Bryon and Amy talking to the secretary. She acted as if she enjoyed their company.

"Let's go," she announced.

She drove to the doctor's office with the directions the secretary gave her. She signed Jenny and Jason in and then they waited. Thirty minutes later, a nurse called them back to a room. Then another nurse came in to take each one's temperatures.

"I brought them in to have their wounds taken care of. I've already talked to Burt Johnson and Robert Lansing. If you have any questions you're to talk to the sheriff himself," Angie explained. "You do know Burt Johnson don't you?"

"Yes ma'am, I know of him," she answered.

"Good, I just don't want you to blame me for this," Angie stated.

Angie undone Jenny's blouse and took it off with her back toward Jason. The nurse's eyes popped wide open as she stared at Jenny's back.

"Oh my Gawd!" she exclaimed.

"Her back, buttocks, and the back of her legs have the same marks. Jason's back looks the same as hers," Angie informed her.

"We need to put them in different rooms," the nurse said. "Would you put her blouse back on please?"

"Okay, but I don't know how it'll go over, they're very scared," Angie told her skeptically.

"It'll be okay, we'll watch them," she assured her.

The doctor checked them over and made notes on their files. Two hours later, they were checked out of the doctor's office and Angie paid the bill. Then they went to get something to eat at McDonalds. Jenny and Jason did not act so scared now. They found out that Angie would take care of them. When they finished eating, they went back to the lawyer's office.

"You find out anything?" Angie inquired.

"Yes, we just came from Judge Russell's chambers. They have a warrant to pick Maggie up. Later this afternoon I'll have some papers for you to sign," he explained. "Can you stay in town two or three hours?"

"Yes of course, as long as it takes," she answered.

"Good, come back about three thirty," he told her.

"Thank you so much," she uttered with a sigh of relief.

"It'll cost you, I'll send you a bill," he said smiling.

"Yes I know, and it'll be worth it. We'll be back later," she said.

Angie stopped at the secretary's desk to ask directions. She needed to get clothes for Jenny and Jason.

"Could you tell me where there's a second hand clothing store here in town?" Angie asked.

"Yes ma'am, go east through town. As you're leaving town there's a store on your left. There's a IGA store across the street," she told her.

"Thank you so much," Angie, said.

"You're welcome," she replied.

They went shopping for clothes most of the afternoon. She brought shirts and pants for both of them, and she found three dresses that would fit Jenny. Then she had to go to a department store to buy underwear for them. Jason did not say anything but he smiled each time Angie spoke to him. All afternoon Jenny made sure that she did not get more than six feet from Angie. When they got back to the lawyer's office, they had to wait for him to come back.

"All of these your children?" the secretary asked.

"These two here are, the other two I'm taking care of," she answered.

"I was just wondering, with four kids you're gonna have your hands full," she mentioned.

"I lost my husband a while back, and with Robert's help I'm getting the estate settled," she told her.

"You'll make it I know you will. I can offer a little help on weekends," she told her.

"Well bless your heart," Angie said surprised. "You know where I live?"

"I can look on your records. I'll find it. My names Sandra," she told her.

"You're so kind. I wish he'd come on," Angie mentioned.

At that moment, the front door opened. Robert walked in with a arm full of papers. He laid the papers down on the desk and sorted out the ones she had to sign. Angie signed the papers granting her temporary custody.

"Thank you so much," Angie, said.

"You're welcome," he told her.

They left the office to go home stopping at the grocery store on the way. The first night would be the worst for them. They acted very withdrawn and they constantly watched Angie. Amy was helping to cook the meal and Jenny wanted to do something. She watched Angie a few minutes and then she held her hands out in front of her.

"You want to help?" Angie inquired.

"Yeah," she uttered.

Angie almost broke down as tears rolled down her cheeks. Jenny was trying so hard. Angie wanted to wipe her tears away but her hands were oily.

"You've got to wash your hands first," she told her.

Jenny quickly washed her hands at the sink and dried them on a hand towel. Now she was ready to help.

"Very good, I'll make a good cook out of you," she said.

"Okay," she agreed.

There must have been a great wrestling inside of them. They knew that they did not have to leave the house. They knew that Angie actually cared for them. If they were with their mother, she would severely beat them. Both of them were tired of being beaten especially when they knew that they never did anything wrong. In a old shed at home is where they spent many nights on a lumpy couch huddled together under a blanket to keep warm. Here lately, they would sleep in the shed a lot so they would not have to listen to their mother scream at them.

"Take the pot off the burner Jenny, use a pot holder so you won't get burnt," Angie told her.

She picked up a potholder and lifted the pot off the burner, and sat it on an iron plate with legs on the counter.

"Very good," Angie said giving her a hug. "Your hands clean Jason?"

"I — don't—," he uttered slowly.

"Come here," she said.

He got up slowly and cautiously walked to Angie. He stopped about a yard from her and waited.

"Hold your hands out," she told him.

He looked at her oddly for a minute and then he held his hands out for her to inspect. She took a hold of his hands and turned them palms up.

"They need washed for supper," she said smiling. "Would you go with him Bryon?"

"Sure Mom," he agreed leading the way to the bathroom.

Jason followed along not sure what to expect. He did not want to get beat. He would rather run off into the hills to be away from people like his mother. Jenny liked it here with Mrs. Bradshaw so he was not going to leave his sister behind.

In a few minutes, they returned from the bathroom. Jason hoped that his hands were clean. What would she do?

"Let's see," Angie, said.

Again, he held out his hands. She pretended to look very closely as if she expected to find a small bug or something. The next thing that she did was much unexpected. She dropped his hands as if they became too heavy, wrapped him up in her arms, and squeezed tightly for a minute. After she released him, he stood with a smile on his face. Now he was confused for sure. Would it come later? The thing that would make him cry before he fell asleep and have nightmares? Too often, his mother beat him that is what caused the nightmares in the middle of the night.

"Very good Jason," Angie told him.

She gave him a hug, and told him that he did well. He just did what she told him to do. What would come later? Would it be a nice surprise? He had thoughts about running away earlier, but now he was not so sure. No one treated him the way Mrs. Bradshaw treated him before today. Then Angie gave Bryon and Amy a hug and a kiss on the forehead. She was very proud of them. Jenny and Jason were learning and Bryon and Amy helped them.

"You can set the table Jason. The plates are in the cupboard," she told him.

He stood with his mouth hanging open for a minute. He had never set a table before. He was scared of breaking a plate. Yes, he had to be very careful. Wow, she trusted him to do something. Finally, he found the right cupboard and carried one plate at a time so he would not break one. Then he stopped when he had four plates on the table.

How many was he supposed to put on the table? Yes, there was Jason, Jenny, Mrs. Bradshaw, and Bryon and Amy. How many was that? He struggled hard for a minute ready to give up almost. He counted on his fingers. There was one finger for each of them including him. He strained hard to get one word out that they would understand.

"Five," he uttered loudly.

"That's right Jason, very good. Get one more plate and don't forget the silverware. A fork, knife, and spoon at each plate," Angie told him.

He walked to the cupboard to get one more plate as Jenny smiled at him. Jenny was putting store bought biscuits on a flat pan to put in the oven to bake. Silverware, where was the silverware? Oh yes, it was in the drawer next to the sink. He put a fork on the left side of each plate, and a table knife and spoon on the right. Then he got five plastic glasses out of the cupboard and filled one glass at a time with ice. The more she allowed him to do the better he felt about himself.

"That's very good Jason, I'm proud of you. As soon as the bread gets done, we'll eat," Angie told him.

He stood smiling at Angie. Their mother never allowed them to help her, but she would holler at them and tell them how worthless they were.

"Watch the bread Jenny. When the bottom gets brown turn the top broiler on to brown the tops," she told her.

"Okay," she said nodding her head.

Maybe it was not going to be as hard as Angie thought. She was not totally sure about Jason. Thankfully, Bryon and Amy accepted them. She did not know if it was open arms willingly or not, but they helped without her telling them. Jenny and Jason were a a little small for their age. When she got the sales straightened out, she was going to take them home with her.

Soon supper was ready and they sat down to eat. Jenny was thrilled beyond words because she got to help. When they finished eating the children washed and dried the dishes and put them away.

"I know what all of you can do," Angie stated.

"What's that Mom?" Amy asked.

"All of you can make cookies," she said.

"Yeah, we get to make cookies," Amy shrieked excitedly. "What can we make Mom?"

"Oh I don't know. Sugar cookies got to be chilled usually. We need to find out what we have," she said.

She found oatmeal, chocolate chips, raisins, and all-purpose flour. She sat all of the ingredients on the counter. Then she remembered seeing a box of recipes in the cupboard. She laid the recipe she wanted on the counter. Jason stood in the doorway feeling left out. The corners of his mouth went down like an upside down letter U. When Angie spoke, he jerked out of his trance.

"Come here Jason," she said.

He slowly walked to where Angie stood and waited for her to quit talking to the girls. His face looked long as he waited.

"Open the door there Jason, and take out two cookie sheets," she said holding up two fingers.

A smile came on his face again because he felt wanted. Yes, he was going to help also. When he took the cookie, sheets out he turned to look at her.

"You'd better wash them first. I don't know how long they've been down there," she told him.

She went to the sink, put in the stopper, and turned on the hot water adding a little soap. When the sink was half-full she shut the water off. She handed a dishcloth to Jason and he stuck both pans in the water. She showed him how to wash them, rinse them off, and put them in the dish drainer.

"Let them dry and then we'll put a little grease on them so the cookies won't stick to the pan," she told him.

He quickly nodded his head. Bryon was helping the girls so they would get the measurements right. They did not want the cookies to be a flop. Soon they had the cookie dough mixed up, and Jason had the pans ready. They put rolled up balls of dough on the sheets and put them in the oven. Jenny watched through the glass window on the oven door to see the cookies bake. It gave her satisfaction to watch something she helped make turn to a golden brown. The real test would come later. Amy and Jenny had flour on their shirts and an imprint of flour from their hands on the seats of their pants.

"Done yet?" Jenny asked.

"No, a few more minutes Jenny," Angie told her.

Jenny turned back to watching through the glass door. She was ready for them to come out. The outer edges had turned to a dark brown. She took the potholder and took the two pans out.

"Get the cooling racks Bryon," she said.

Bryon put the racks on the counter, got a spatula, and lifted the cookies off to put them on the racks. When he finished the girls put more cookie dough on the pans to bake.

"Let them cool," Angie suggested.

Ten minutes later, she took a cookie and took a bite. She tried to keep a straight face as they watched her intently.

"Wow, they're wonderful. They really taste good," she said, as Jenny got excited.

"You really think so?" Jenny asked.

"Yes of course Jenny," she said as she hugged her.

"I help," Jason said.

"Yes you did, all of you did a good job," she said, as she hugged Jason, Amy, and Bryon.

"Before you eat all the cookies wait a minute," Angie said. "Who wants cocoa?"

"I do," all of them answered.

6

For the next two weeks, everything went along smoothly. Jenny and Jason were adjusting fine. They would still get set in an act to rebellion or hard- headedness. Angie would hold them in her arms until they calmed down. The first time she had to catch Jason and hold him until he felt assured that she was there to take care of him. They still could picture how their mother treated them and they rebelled.

Angie did not realize at the time what kind of challenge she was letting herself in for with them. At first, they were very hard to handle, and their moods would flare up occasionally. They only asked about their parents once. Their father still had not come home yet. The welts on their backs and almost healed fully. They were going to have scars on their skin and scars inside. Jenny turned out to have an overflowing heart of love for Angie and her children. Each day Jenny wanted at least one hug. Jason still had trouble expressing himself although he was slowly getting better. He could say more than one word at a time now.

One day Angie dressed Jenny up in a dress. Jenny acted very nervous, as Angie looked her up and down. She put light pink lipstick on Jenny's lips, and then she used eyeliner and make up on her.

"Tell me what you think," Angie said.

"It's nice Mom," she said with a shaky voice.

"Thank you, let's go show the others," she suggested.

Jenny bashfully followed Angie into the living room where the other children sat. Jenny was very nervous.

"What you think Amy," her mother asked.

"Wow," she uttered as she stared at Jenny.

"Who that?" Jason asked.

"Your sister silly," Angie said giggling.

"No she ain't," Jason insisted.

"She's pretty Mom," Amy said.

"That's your sister Jason," Angie told him again.

"She don't look it," he said slowly.

"Do you want to wear that today," Angie, asked her.

"Yes please," Jenny answered.

"Keep your legs together when you sit down," she suggested.

"Okay," she said nodding her head.

Jenny walked over, sat down beside Bryon, and crossed her arms firmly. She was perturbed because her brother did not recognize her, his own sister.

"You smell nice," Bryon said softly.

"Thank you," she told him.

Jason would often stare at his sister not believing his eyes. Her face always looked the same before today, and now he was not so sure.

"I made her look pretty Jason," Angie said.

"She look different," he insisted.

"Well of course Jason," she said. "Don't you want your sister to look pretty?"

"Tell him Mom," Jenny stated loudly.

"Well yeah I guess," he said slowly.

"She needs a small handbag, a perm, high heels, and he won't know his sister for sure," Amy said giggling.

"Not funny," Jason stated.

"No it's not funny. Don't tease him, they've been through enough," Angie told them. "Would you like to have a suit Jason?"

"Suit of what?" he asked.

"Just a minute Jason," she told him.

Angie walked to her bedroom to get a catalog from J. C. Pennys. She thumbed through until she got to the boys clothes. There she found a picture of a boy in a two-piece suit.

"Like this Jason," she said pointing. "See the boy in a suit?"

"Yeah I guess," he told her perking up a little.

"You think Jenny would know who you were dressed like that?" she asked.

"I don't know," he said.

"Regardless how you look on the outside Jason, what really matters is what comes from in there," she said tapping him on his chest.

"Yes ma'am," he said.

"Children, do you know we don't have a cookie in the house? Who wants to make cookies?" Angie asked.

"I do," he hollered out.

"They almost ran into the kitchen to get started. They knew what to do including Jason. He got the pans out, washed them, dried them, and put a light coat of grease on each one.

Jenny had never had someone treat her like this before in her life. Now she felt like someone that belonged to someone instead of a drug addict's child. Now she had a chance to be a young woman. Angie made sure that she felt like a young lady, her hair was growing back and Jenny felt good about herself. Every day Angie taught them math, English, history, and how to conduct themselves. More than once Angie had to hold them to keep them from acting wild. They were a challenge for Angie, and holding them tightly was the best way for her to calm them down. Jason struggled free a couple of times and she had to use all of her strength to hold him still.

By the end of June, two of the other store renters arranged to buy. The last two wanted to wait until the end of the year. Out of the sales, she had to pay inheritance taxes. It took almost everything she had leaving her with very little. Twice a year she would have money coming in from the leases up in the hills. Every month she had money coming in from the six places in town.

One day while Angie was at the grocery store, Hazel introduced her to an elderly woman. Hazel had her reasons. She knew that the woman could tell Angie about her husband.

"Hello, she said.

"Hello, I'm Angie Bradshaw."

"My name's Abigail Crabtree."

"She was married to William Bradshaw," Hazel mentioned.

"Aw yes, I remember him," Abigail said.

"You knew him?" Angie asked surprised.

"Yes as a child. He'd come up here to spend the summer with Morgan every year until he was about fifteen years old. From what I heard, they had a falling out of some kind. I never knew all the details myself. All I know is one day William got on the bus and never came back," Abigail explained.

"I wonder what happened. William never said a word about coming up here. Now my curiosity's aroused," Angie, uttered.

"I know someone that knows if you're interested," she suggested.

"Yes of course I'm interested," she gasped.

"I'll tell her about you," Abigail mentioned.

"Yes please do. I've wondered a long time what the connection was," Angie said in deep thought.

"When I see her I'll tell her," she said.

"Thank you so much," Angie stated.

"You're welcome, see ya later," Abigail said.

Angie watched her shuffle down the isle. Then she paid for her purchases and left to go home.

That evening Angie called her sister Helen, to check on things. She had not talked to her since she left home. She should have called her before now that there was so many things going on.

"Hello."

"Hello, this is Angie," she told her.

"Where you been for over a month?" Helen asked very worried.

"Here in Hagon's Bluff," she answered.

"So what'd you inherit?" Helen inquired.

"There's six stores in town I'm trying to sell. Up in the hills there's two hundred and fifty acres that ten families live on. I live in a two-story house that sits on forty acres. I got a Ford pickup, and three old cars," she explained.

"Wow, you're set for life!" Helen exclaimed.

"Not quite, the inheritance tax ate a big hole in my pocket," she told her.

"I'll bet it did with all of that," she agreed.

"I also got two more kids to raise. Their mother was on hard drugs when she gave birth to them. They have their ways caused by the drugs but we're working on that problem. They're adjusting slowly. As soon as I get some rent payments I'll be down," Angie explained.

"I never figured you'd do something like that Angie," she uttered.

"They came to the house hungry with welts on their backs from being beaten. Twice the girl was bleeding where she was beaten," she stated. "What was I supposed to do ignore them?"

"Oh no, I didn't know they were beaten," Helen said gasping.

"They were, their backs are healed now with several scars," she told her.

"I don't know what to say Angie," she uttered. "They both boys?"

"A boy and a girl, they're twins. They have blonde hair, and hazel eyes. The girl's hair was cut short like a boys, and I'll give her a perm when it gets some length. It'll tear your heart out to be around them and listen. I work with them everyday and sometimes we've got to go over things several times. Amy and Bryon helps them a lot," she explained.

"What you teaching them?" asked Helen.

"Math, English, reading, and writing," she answered.

"Don't they go to school?" she inquired.

"They will this fall. Before then I'm not sure what happened. Before I got them they didn't know what it was like to be a child," she answered.

"Sounds like you got your hands full," she mentioned. "Where do you live?"

"In Morgan Bradshaw's house. It's a two-story house with four bedrooms. Amy and Jenny takes turns sleeping with me," she answered.

"What's their names?" Helen inquired.

"Jenny and Jason."

"I'd better get off of here Sis. Come and see me soon," she suggested.

"I will, love you," she said.

"Love you Angie," Helen replied.

"I gave you my phone number didn't I?" Angie asked.

"Yeah, I got it," she answered.

"Good, I'll talk to you later," she replied.

"Good bye Sis."

Later she remembered that she never asked Helen about the house. Well she had to get moved soon anyway. A few days later, she went to the lawyer again. He was in Court this morning but she expected him to be free this afternoon. Then she walked back to the car deciding what to do.

"He's not in, so I guess we'll go shopping," she stated.

"Where we going," Bryon asked.

"I don't know, we've got to kill some time," she answered.

They found a shopping mall and went inside to look around. They looked in several stores looking at several things that she did not want to buy. For lunch, they had nachos and a cheese sauce at a little Taco Bell. At one thirty, they went back to the lawyer's office.

"May I help you Mrs. Bradshaw?" Robert asked.

"I'd like permanent custody of Jenny and Jason," she said.

"We'll have to work on that. I need consent of at least one parent. I don't know how to get in touch with Mr. Thompkins. I can go see Maggie and see what she says. I doubt if she'll do anything except talk hateful," he explained.

"It's hard to get medicade or anything else for them. The inheritance tax about drained my resources," she stated firmly.

"I'll see what I can do," he said.

"Please do. I'm gonna take them with me when I go home," she mentioned.

"You're coming back are you not?" Robert inquired.

"Yes sir, let me know what you find out," she said.

"I'll try, but I feel that it's a waste of my time to go see her. I'll see what I can do," he assured her.

"Thank you so much for your time," she said getting up to go.

She got the children and went home. She had to take one day at a time. A week later, a stranger knocked on the door.

"May I help you?" she asked.

"You got my kids?" the man asked.

"Stay right there a minute," she said closing the door.

She ran upstairs to get Jenny and Jason. Angie looked very worried as she got them together. He wanted to see them. Did they want to see him?

"Your father's outside," she told them. "Do you want to see him?"

"I guess," Jenny muttered.

"He okay," Jason said.

"Do you want to see him?" she asked again.

"As long as he don't take us away," Jennie said fearfully.

"He can't do that unless I agree," Angie stated.

"Okay," they agreed.

Angie went back to the front door and opened it wide. She stood looking at him a moment wondering why he showed up now.

"Come in Mr. Thompkins. I want you to know up front I've got legal custody of Jenny and Jason. I've been through a rough time with them," she told him sternly.

"I'm not here to take them, I just want to see them," he said quickly.

"Okay, and then what?" Angie asked worried.

"They told me about you getting everything here. I wanted to meet you so I could pay you the lease money. I do want to see my kids though," he explained.

No one was in the living room except Angie and Mr. Thompkins. She knew that they were not anxious about coming down. They were a little afraid to see him.

"Come on down children," Angie hollered.

Jenny and Jason followed Bryon and Amy down the stairs slowly. They were very leery about being around their father after living with Angie. He had never beaten them like their mother, but he did not spend much time with them.

"Here they are," she told him.

"Great day they've changed! You've done a good job with them," he said almost in tears.

"They're loved and cared for now. I've been teaching them everything I can so they'll be ready for school this fall," she told him.

"They used to go to school until they were about ten. I gave Maggie a lot of money so they could go to school for the underdeveloped. I don't know what she did with the money, she wouldn't tell me. I can guess what she did. I've been away so much making a living so they'd have something. I should of know better that to marry her in the first place," he told them.

"Would you give me the right to have full custody of them?" she asked. "That way you could have visitation rights."

"I reckon that'd be the best thing to do or I'll have to pay child support," he said nodding his head.

"That's right Mr. Thompkins," she said firmly. "You seen your wife?"

"Yeah for a minute. She sounds so hateful toward you for taking her youngins' away," he said.

"They came to the house with welts on their backs from a leather belt. They were beaten from their shoulders to their knees. Jenny came to the house twice with her back bleeding," she told him firmly.

"Yeah, I knew she did that a little," he mentioned.

"A little!" Angie exclaimed loudly.

He stood looking at the floor for a long minute. Then he started to say something but Angie cut him off.

"Look here Mr. Thompkins. The second time she came to the house with blood on her back I did something. I didn't let it go on just because I knew about it. They don't need to live that kind of life. I went to my lawyer, talked to the sheriff, and took them to the doctor. Judge Russell gave me temporary custody. I'd like to get full custody of them so I can get medicade for them. They need to make regular doctor visits. They'll have to go to a special school until they get caught up on their studies," she explained firmly.

"If you get full custody will I get to see them?" he asked unsure.

"Yes sir, I already told you that," she answered.

"Let's do it then," he suggested.

"How long you gonna be in town?" she inquired.

"A month or more," he answered.

"All right, we'll go see my lawyer tomorrow," she told him. "Okay?"

"Yes ma'am," he answered. "What time you want to leave?"

"Tomorrow morning. Wait a minute, I'd better call first," she answered. "Want some coffee?"

"Yes please. I've worked construction jobs all my life, that's all I know. It's a heck of a life but a lot of folks do it now days. I'm not making excuses, I just wanted you to know," he told her.

"It's okay," she said.

"How'd you end up with all of this?" he asked.

"It was willed to my husband, but he passed away two months ago," she answered.

"I'm so sorry to hear it ma'am. I was just curious. Anyway, here's the money for the lease," he told her. "You reckon I could get a receipt?"

"Yes sir, I can do that," she agreed.

She wrote out a receipt and gave it to him. Then she called the lawyers office. It rang several times before someone answered. Then she hung up when Sandra told her.

"He won't be in until one thirty, so we'll leave about twelve thirty I guess," she told him.

"Okay, I'll bring their clothes over tomorrow. Give me a hug kids I'll be back tomorrow. I've got a bunch of cleaning to do," he told them.

Jenny and Jason went to their father and gave him a hug. They had not seen him for five months. Then they went back, stood beside Angie, and watched. In a few minutes, he left the house to go home.

"Let's go to town kids," Angie suggested.

The children nodded their heads and headed for the car. She wanted to stop at the garage for a minute. She parked in front and got out.

"Hey Mrs. Bradshaw," he said nodding his head.

"Good morning, I wanted to know when you was coming over," she said.

"I hope to next week," Ben, told her.

"Who's truck sitting there," Angie inquired.

"Mine, it's got a twenty five foot bed," he answered.

"Does it run good," she asked.

"Yeah, come and listen to it. It's got a diesel engine with a turbo in it," he stated.

She followed him out to the truck. He opened the door and stood on the running board. Then he turned the key to the start position and the engine came to life. He let it run a minute and then he shut it off.

"What you gonna do with it?" she inquired.

"I reckon keep it, I ain't for sure," he answered.

"If I give you the money for license and insurance can I borrow it?" she asked him.

"What you gonna do with it?" he inquired.

"Move up here," she replied.

"Yeah, I reckon you can Mrs. Bradshaw," he said nodding his head.

"I gotta have something to move with," she stated firmly.

"I'll do it Mrs. Bradshaw," he agreed.

Angie handed him three hundred dollars. She knew the license tags would not cost much, but the insurance would. She just hoped that she was not making a mistake.

"When you want it ready?" he asked.

"In a week, no more than two," she answered.

"I'll do it ma'am. I think I got one of your cars sold. I gotta make another phone call," he told her.

"That's great, sell all three of them for a high dollar," she said.

"I'm working on it ma'am," he stated.

"I'll check back with you," she told him.

"Okay," he agreed.

Angie walked out to the car and drove off. They stopped at the grocery store for the girls. They wanted to make a cake. They wanted a cake mix and frosting to put on it.

The next day about eleven thirty Mr. Thompkins came to the house. He carried in two big cardboard boxes into the house filled with Jenny and Jason's clothes. He sat one down and carried in the other box. Bryon and Jason carried the boxes upstairs to their rooms.

"Would you help me move Mr. Thompkins?" she asked. "You said you was gonna be around for a while."

"Yeah sure, I can help you," he answered. "When you wanna go?"

"In a week or two. Mr. Ben's got to get the truck ready," she answered.

"Okay, sounds good to me," he agreed.

"Let's go to town," Angie suggested.

When they got to the lawyer's office, they went inside. Sandra was sitting at the desk talking to someone on the phone. She did not look pleased at all. Five minutes later, she hung the phone up.

"May I help you Mrs. Bradshaw?" Sandra asked.

"I'd like to see Robert please," she said.

"Come on back, he's expecting you," she told her.

"Stay here children, we'll be back in a few minutes," Angie told them.

She walked down the hall with Ralph following behind. She stopped in the doorway and waited. Soon he looked up to see who was there waiting.

"Good afternoon Mrs. Bradshaw," Robert said.

"Good afternoon, this is Ralph Thompkins. He said he'd give me full custody of the children as long as he has visitation rights. This is fine with me," she explained.

"Is that right Mr. Thompkins?" Robert inquired.

"Yes sir, that'd be the right thing to do for the children. With Maggie in jail, I can't take care of them properly. As you found out Maggie hasn't been taking care of them. I know Mrs. Bradshaw will take good care of the children," he explained.

"Okay, that's all I need to know. Come back day after tomorrow at two p. m. and I'll have the papers ready for both of you to sign," he told them.

"Thank you so much," Angie uttered.

"Are you aware Mr. Thompkins you'd be liable for child support if you don't agree to these terms?" Robert inquired.

"Yes sir, I know," he answered.

"Good, I'll have the papers drawn up and present them to Judge Russell. He's already aware of what's going on. I'll put the stipulation in that you've got visitation rights," he explained.

"Thank you sir, I just want what's best for the children," he said.

"Yes sir," he agreed.

"Thank you so much, we'll see you in two days," Angie told him.

They left the office with Angie feeling excited. She got what she wanted and now the children could feel safe and secure. Now she had to get them registered for school.

"You want to do anything while we're in town Mr. Thompkins?" Angie asked.

"No ma'am," he answered.

"You don't want to see Maggie?" she inquired.

"No ma'am, I don't want to hear that hateful mouth. She's the one that did wrong," he told her.

"Yes, but you allowed it," she stated.

"Yeah I know, and it's time to stop. I want those nightmares behind me," he said sternly.

"I'd like for you to take me up in the hills and introduce me to the people that live there," she told him. "You got time to do that?"

"Yes ma'am," he answered. "You wanna do that today?"

"Yes sir if possible," she said.

"If I can remember where all of them live," he uttered.

7

She drove back to Hagon's Bluff and down the road toward the hills. The first place was Ralph Thompkins place. The second place they came to was the Rawlings place. Angie drove up the driveway and stopped near the house. Angie and Ralph got out and walked to the house. He knocked on the door and then they waited. Soon the door opened and a middle-aged woman stood looking at them.

"What ya doing Ralph? Got a new girlfriend?" she asked with a sneer.

"No ma'am, this be Mrs. Bradshaw; she's your new landlord. She inherited everything here including this land," he told her sternly.

"Oh my goodness, I'm so sorry. Please come in," she said holding the door open.

They followed her to the back of the house to the kitchen where a man sat at the table drinking coffee. He had graying hair at the temples.

"Honey, this here be Angie Bradshaw our new landlord," she told him.

He quickly stood up and shook her hand. He wore bib overalls with a tee shirt underneath.

"Please sit down ma'am," he said. "How ya been getting on Ralph?"

"Working all the time. I'm off for forty-five days now," he said.

"Well it's good to see ya again," he told him.

"Since I'm home she wanted me to introduce her to the people up here," he explained.

"That's good Ralph, I was a wondering what was a gonna take place. Old Morgan was something else," Mr. Rawlings said. "What you gonna do with all of this Mrs. Bradshaw?"

"Up here, I'm going to leave it like it is. In town, the businesses want to buy the places they're renting. I don't know why Morgan didn't want to sell to them," Angie explained.

"So's he could keep 'em under his thumb. Those poor people didn't have any say if they was renting," Mr. Rawlings said.

"When's your lease up?" Angie asked.

"In twenty-ten with the option to renew," he said.

"What about buying?" Angie asked. "That way the place would be yours. I've got no arguments with that."

"Well bless your heart," Mr. Rawlings uttered.

"What's your name's?" Angie inquired.

"I'm Bessie and he's Bill," she answered.

"I lost my husband two months ago due to cancer," Angie mentioned.

"I'm so sorry Mrs. Bradshaw," Bessie said.

"Cancer hey?" Bill asked. "There's a lot of that going around. Even the youngins' a dying of cancer. When I was a youngin' it was consumption. It's just a name for something they don't know how to cure."

"We'd better get on," Ralph mentioned.

"Please come back again Mrs. Bradshaw," Bessie suggested.

"I will," she told her.

Then they left to go to the rest of the places. It was about five o'clock in the afternoon when they got to the last place. A big-boned woman came to the door. She was not plump, but she stood at least six foot tall.

"May I help you?" she asked.

"My name's Angie Bradshaw. I came up to talk to you a while," she answered.

"What's it about?" she asked.

"I'm your new landlord," Angie stated. "You knew Morgan passed on didn't you?"

"Yes ma'am, I heard about it later. Please come in," she said holding the door open.

Then she led them back to the kitchen where she had just started supper. She had a lot to do by herself.

"While Mr. Thompkins is in town I asked him to show me where all the renters lived," she told her.

"I've heard about Maggie Thompkins," she mentioned.

"That's my wife. I work construction jobs so I'm not home much. Mrs. Bradshaw's got a heavy load to tote to get Morgan's mess straightened out. Her husband died of cancer before she came up here," Ralph explained.

"I declare, you've had it rough. I want all of you to stay for supper," she told them.

"There's four kids out in the car," Angie said worried.

"So what?" she asked. "Bring em'in."

"You sure?" Angie asked.

"I declare, yes of course, ya'll welcome," she stated.

"I'll get em'," Ralph suggested.

"Great day, I'm so glad to meet ya. I was wondering what we was a gonna do. Any news that reaches up here tis about a week old," she told her. "What'd ya say your name was?"

"Angie Bradshaw. My husband was William and everyone called him Bill," she told her. "You sure you got food for all of us?"

"Lordy yes, you're welcome," she assured her. "Did you husband come up here in the summers?"

"Yes, Mrs. Crabtree told me he came up here every summer until he was about fifteen years old. Then one day he got on the bus and never came back," Angie explained.

"If I remember right I know what the deal was," she mentioned.

"Yes, what was it?" What's your name?" Angie asked.

"How old was your husband?" she inquired. "My name's Ann and my husband is Frank."

"He was thirty-five this year," she answered.

"I declare that's it. Everything fits together. He was in love with Lucy Cummings he was. Oh Lordy, she was a looker when she was young. When Morgan found out about the new love affair, he forbid him to see her. Her parents were poor dirt farmers. Morgan had his standards on a so called moral ladder. If ya wasn't high society like he thought he was, the lower class didn't fit in. Wealth don't make ya happy but I reckon you already know that," Ann explained.

"I was trying to figure out what the connection was between Morgan and William," Angie said.

"It was his first love Lucy was. She lives across the holler from us. I reckon ten miles as a crow flies," Ann told her.

"I'd like to meet her," Angie suggested.

"You wouldn't want to ma'am. Drugs and alcohol ain't done her no justice," she stated.

"Oh really?" she asked.

"You don't do any of that do ya?" she asked.

"No ma'am, neither one," Angie stated.

"That's good; it always ends up to the bad. I gotta finish supper," Ann told her.

"Need some help?" Angie asked.

"Yeah I reckon I do," she answered.

They cooked supper together, and an hour later, they were ready for everyone to eat. Ann and her husband had four children. Angie set twelve places at the table. After supper, Angie helped wash the dishes, and clean up the kitchen.

"I declare, you'd never seen Morgan eating at my table. He was a good man in many ways, but the things he'd be a doing I didn't cotton to," Ann explained.

"Yeah, I've heard various stories," Angie committed.

"What you reckon you'll do?" she asked.

"Stay up here. I'm a gonna move up here in a couple of weeks. I like it up here. The kids been talking about going camping," Angie told her.

"That's what my kids been talking about. The cows don't have to be fed this time of year. I declare, when ya get moved let's go camping. I know a nice campground about thirty miles from here. The kids can go fishing and hiking," Ann suggested.

"That sounds like a good idea. We'd better get home soon it's dark outside. Thank you so much for everything," Angie told her.

She got the kids together, found Ralph, and left to go home. Ralph went home as soon as she parked the car. When they got inside, she told the children to take baths and get ready for bed.

A week later, Ben had the moving van ready. They left the next morning to go to Lancaster. They had to spend one night in a motel room. Ralph and the boys stayed in one room and Angie and the girls stayed in the next room. That afternoon they arrived at Angie's home. Ralph backed the truck up the driveway and stopped near the garage. Angie unlocked the house for everyone to go inside to get things ready.

8

The next morning Angie called her sister for her to come over. Angie did not know what she was going to do with all of this stuff. Most of it she would take back, and some of it she would give away.

Jenny was in a strange environment so she stayed close to Angie. She would carry a box out to the truck and then she would run back to be with Angie. Wherever Jenny was Jason was nearby.

An hour later, Helen came to the house. Her children were not with her today.

"It's about time you made it Sis," she said hugging Angie.

"Hi Helen, it's good to see you. This is Jenny and Jason. I told you about them. This is Ralph Thompkins, their father. I've got full custody of them, and he's got visitation rights when he's in town," she explained.

"They're nice looking kids," Helen said. "How's Bryon and Amy?"

"We're good," Bryon said.

"Hi Aunt Helen," Amy told her.

"I'm glad my powers still on," Angie mentioned.

"You sure you want to live so far away?" Helen inquired.

"You're not married; you could come up and stay with us. You'd like it up there. I don't know what it's like in the winter time though, it probably gets cold," she told her. "Did you know William went up there to stay with Morgan?"

"I had no idea," she uttered.

"He went up there until he was fifteen. I know we've got to find some boxes," she told her.

Angie, Jenny, and Jason left to find boxes at several stores. They took the boxes apart, folded them up, and stacked them in the car. Jason would climb into the dumpster to get the boxes out. Then they stopped at the hardware store to get several rolls of duct tape.

The next day Angie sister Tammy came over to help her pack. She brought her two boys with her. Angie had not seen her nephews for two years. Tammy was driving an old car that the fenders had several dents.

"What you been doing Tammy?" Helen asked.

"We ain't seen you for ages," Angie said.

"Trying to get back on my feet. I divorced my husband the fool. I caught him in bed with some hussy," she told them.

"Oh no, I hate to hear about that Tammy," Angie stated.

"It's water under the bridge now," Tammy replied.

Two hours later, they were busy packing boxes, and Ralph was out in the back yard cleaning out the shed. Suddenly Jenny came running into the bedroom where Angie was working.

"They're fighting Mom," Jenny said between sobs.

"Who's fighting?" Angie asked.

"Jason and two boys," she answered.

Angie ran outside to see Jason beating both of Tammy's boys. Then the youngest boy turned and ran toward the house holding his hand over his face as blood oozed out between his fingers. A minute later, the other boy lay on the grass doubled up holding his stomach. Angie ran to Jason and led him back to the house looking him over to see if he was hurt.

Jason was very worried about being beat with a belt. That is what his mother did when the principal kicked them out of school for Jason defending Jenny. He was doing the same thing today, defending Jenny.

"What's going on here?" Angie asked.

"They called us a stupid retard along with other names. When we wouldn't move out of their way, they shoved me down. They tried to shove Jason down. Then I came in to get you," Jenny explained.

Jenny showed Angie her hands and her elbow. Blood started

seeping out where the concrete peeled her skin roughly. She held her arm because of the pain.

"They deserve to be beat," Bryon commented.

"What's going on?" Tammy asked as she came up.

"Your boys called them a stupid retard and other names. Then they shoved Jenny down on the sidewalk," Angie told her angrily.

"So?" she asked. "Their playing got out of hand."

"Out of hand my rear end!" she exclaimed loudly.

Tammy stood looking at her sister in shock. She did not know what to say. She knew that her boys played rough at times.

"This was deliberate Tammy, look at her," Angie told her firmly.

Angie showed Tammy Jenny's arms and hands. Tammy's eyes became big as she looked closely. The little girl did not deserve shoved down.

Angie took Jenny and Jason to the bathroom to get them cleaned up. She washed Jenny's hands and arms and used peroxide where the skin remained peeled loose. One place on Jenny's elbow her blood seeped out she put a bandage over the wound. Ralph came in the house while Angie cleaned Jenny's arm.

"What's been going on?" he asked surprised.

"Jason just beat the stuffing out of two boys that shoved Jenny down on the sidewalk," Angie stated.

"Well I'll be," he uttered. "You two okay?"

"I did my best Dad," Jason told him.

"He said they got kicked out of school once because he defended Jenny," Angie mentioned.

"Well I'll be. You do your best is all I ask," Ralph said.

Jason felt good about himself in a way. Angie did not want him to get into a scrap at the drop of a hat, but she did not want him to back down either. Jason was glad that Angie did not wildly beat him with a belt for defending his sister.

"What brought this on?" Angie asked.

"We carried boxes out to the truck when they started in on us. They kept pushing Jason with their hands. When they pushed me down Jason started beating them," Jenny explained.

"I'm afraid I gave my sister a earful. She said their playing got out of hand and I blew up at her," she told Ralph.

"Well, maybe it's for the best," Ralph, mentioned.

They went back to the bedroom and continued packing boxes. A few minutes later, Tammy came in the room to talk to Angie. She was still mad as she stood holding her hands together.

"I'm gonna take those two home," Tammy mentioned.

"Okay, take care Tammy," Angie said.

"Where'd you get those two?" Tammy asked.

"If those two hellish boys of yours been through half of what they'd been through they'd be insane," Angie told her with a touch of venom.

"I think he broke Dan's nose," Tammy remarked.

"Well he asked for what he got," Angie told her.

"Why?" she asked. "Those two ain't yours."

"I beg your pardon. No I didn't give birth to them but legally they're mine. I have papers stating so," Angie said firmly.

"I had no idea," Tammy uttered.

"I've been through a lot with them. Next time you'd better find out the facts first," Angie told her.

"I'm so sorry Angie," she muttered.

"Apologize to them. Better yet, your boys ought to apologize to them," Angie suggested.

"Just a minute," Tammy said leaving the room.

Angie told Jenny and Jason to stay put. She did not want any more trouble. Bryon and Amy were busy packing their things in their rooms. Ten minutes later, Tammy returned to the room with her boys. She stood in front of her boys looking very angry.

"Apologize to them," she said firmly.

"I ain't a gonna apologize to no retard," Ray said sarcastically.

Tammy swung her arm around and slapped Ray in the face. Ray staggered backwards bumping into the door staring at his mother.

"Apologize now, both of you!" she exclaimed loudly.

"I'm sorry," Ray, said rubbing his cheek.

"I apologize," Dan, told them.

"Okay, we accept," Jenny, said.

"See you later Angie, I'm sorry things turned out this way," she said.

"Okay, thank you for your help," Angie, said.

"You're welcome," she replied.

Four days later, they had the truck loaded and ready to go. Angie went to the reality office and had the house put on the market. Then she went to the telephone and power company to have their services disconnected. They stayed in a motel room for the night and left early the next morning. When they got home, Ralph parked the truck in front of the garage and left to go home.

The next day she called all of the people in the hills to see if they wanted any of the furniture in the house. Then she called Ben at his garage to let him know she was home.

Then she had the children get in the pickup and they went to Tabor's Point. Angie bought a gas grill, a box of chicken, a box of pork chops, and several pounds of hamburger meat and hot dogs. She hoped that the old freezer at home worked.

When they got home, she cleaned the freezer, plugged it in, and put the meat inside. Then they went out to the garage to put the gas grill together. That evening she called the people back in the hills and told them that she was cooking for everyone Saturday afternoon about one o'clock.

Saturday morning Angie and the children put up four canopy's and put tables under them. They put several small tables inside the garage. Ann and her husband came early so she could help Angie.

"How you doing Angie?" Ann asked.

"Oh fine. I was trying to get al of this started," she answered.

"I declare, I'll help ya," she stated.

"Could you get some ice Frank?" Angie asked.

"Yes ma'am," he answered.

"Take my pickup," she told him.

"Okay," he agreed.

Angie handed him the keys and thirty dollars. The gas grill was almost hot enough to start cooking. She already had the chicken and chops seasoned. Ann was making hamburger patties. She told Jason to get a big metal tub off the back porch and Set it down in the doorway of the garage. The boys put several cans of Pepsi, Mountain Dew, Coke, and Sprite in the tub.

By one o'clock, there were several people there. Angie was worried if there would be enough food. Most of the people brought something to add to what Angie was cooking. There was plenty of potato salad, macaroni and cheese, vegetables, pies, and cakes. She hoped that this would turn out to be a yearly event.

Jenny handed out plates, Jason got drinks for the people, Bryon helped serve food, and Amy handed out napkins and silverware. Some of the people left as soon as they ate, but most of them stayed to visit with Angie.

September second they left the house early so Angie could take the children to school. They found the office down the hall on the right and walked inside. A brown-headed woman looked up as they came in the door.

"Yes ma'am, may I help you?" she asked.

"I need to register four children for school. They told me at the school office I had to wait until school started," Angie told her.

"That's unusual, but we can do it," she said. "What are their names?"

"Bryon Bradshaw, he's twelve. He was born September twentieth nineteen eighty three. Amy Bradshaw is ten, she was born May twentieth nineteen eighty-five. Jenny and Jason were born October second, nineteen eighty-three. Last year Bryon and Amy went to school in Lancaster, North Carolina. Jenny and Jason went to school in this county," she explained.

"We'll have to transfer their records. Now Jenny and Jason will be put in Miss Teasdale's class," she said.

"Can I sit in their class for a while?" Angie inquired.

"I'm sure it'll be all right with her," she answered.

She took Bryon and Amy to their classes, and then she came back for Jenny and Jason. Angie sat in the back of the class so that they would not feel totally lost. She went to lunch with Jenny and Jason and when they got back, Miss Teasdale took their quiz papers back to Angie.

"Have you been teaching them at home during the summer?" she asked.

"Yes I did," Angie, answered.

"It shows, they'll fit in very well," she assured her.

"I'm overwhelmed; that's a big relief," Angie uttered.

"You did a good job," Miss Teasdale said.

"Thank you so much," Angie said. "Do they ride the bus?"

"Where do you live?' she asked.

"In Hagon's Bluff," she answered.

"Yes, but I don't know which one they'll ride," she answered.

"I'll find out," Angie mentioned.

"Did you adopt them?" she asked.

"Yes, I have full custody. I've been through a lot with them," she told her.

"That's good," she uttered.

"Thank you so much for your help," Angie said.

"Oh you're most welcome," Miss Teasdale said.

Angie went to the office to find out about the bus schedule. She wrote the bus number on two sheets of paper and went back to the class.

"Can I interrupt a minute?" Angie asked.

"Yes of course," she answered.

She handed one paper to Jenny and the other to Jason. They looked at them oddly a minute.

"Make sure you get on the bus with that number," she said.

"Okay," Jenny uttered.

"Got it Jason?" she asked.

"Yes Mom," he said.

"I'll see you later," she told them.

She left the class and drove straight back to the house. This was the first time that they were without her. They ought to be home about four she thought.

That evening when the children got home she helped them with their homework.

When they finished they were free to play until suppertime.

Over the next few weeks, Jenny and Jason worked hard to keep their grades up at a B or a C. In social studies, Jenny got an A, and Jason became envious. They were learning. Angie felt very proud of them because they were trying so hard. When the children were in school, she almost felt at a loss. She worked at getting the house the way she wanted it to be. She had time to finally take a deep breath and relax. Up until now, it was one thing after another that went on; getting the furniture moved in, the house arranged, and she gave away all the furniture so there was room for her things.

9

Two months later on a Wednesday, Bryon and Amy came running home from the bus stop out of breath. They waited a minute to catch their breath.

"Jenny and Jason never got on the bus Mom," Bryon uttered.

"Where are they?" she asked very worried.

"I don't know. We looked for them until the bus was ready to leave," he told her.

"Get in the car, we're going to find out why," she said firmly.

She drove to the school in Tabor's Point as fast as she dared. When they got there the school, office was still open but the woman there did not know anything. Then Angie and the children left the school and she drove to the sheriff's office. When she got there, she was a nervous wreck as they walked inside.

"Burt Johnson here?" Angie inquired.

"Yes," a young deputy said. "What's your name?"

"Angie Bradshaw and this is an emergency," she stated almost out of control.

"Just a minute," he said walking away.

A few minutes later, Burt came out of his office to talk to Angie. He looked haggard and tired today.

"Jenny and Jason Thompkins never came home this afternoon on the school bus. I want you to find out where they were taken. Bryon and Amy couldn't find them anywhere before the bus left. I want my children sir," she stated.

"The standard procedure is to start looking after twenty four hours," Burt told her. "What's the teacher's name?"

"Miss Teasdale is all I know," she answered. "Please won't you try?"

"Let me make some phone calls," Burt told her. "You still got temporary custody?"

"No, I have full custody of them. Legally they're mine," she stated firmly.

"Okay," he said.

"They could be out of the state in twenty-four hours," she stated.

"We'll find them Mrs. Bradshaw," he assured her.

"Billy, see if you can find Mrs. Teasdale," Burt said.

"Yes sir," he replied.

"You can wait here until we talk to her," Burt told her.

"Okay, thank you," Angie, said.

They sat down while Angie worried frantically. An hour later, Burt got a call from Betty Teasdale. He talked for several minutes with her before he hung the phone up.

"You had reason for alarm Mrs. Bradshaw. A man and a woman took them out of class at three o'clock. They told her that they now had custody of the children. She got their names, and phone number. I believe she got their address too. They're from Ashland Pennsylvania," he explained.

"You gonna go get them?" Angie asked.

"The authorities will be alerted to pick them up," he said firmly.

"I hope they lock them up in jail. They need to be charged with kidnapping," she said with a touch of venom. "That's what they did ain't it?"

"Yes ma'am," he answered. "Is that what you want?"

"Yes sir, by all means. I want my children back as soon as possible!" she exclaimed.

"We'll try ma'am. I'll request that they put up road blocks," he told her.

"We'll be back sir. We're going to get something to eat," Angie mentioned.

"Okay, we'll be here," he said.

"Let's go kids," she said getting up.

They left the sheriff's office and Angie drove uptown. They stopped at McDonalds and went inside. Bryon and Amy liked cheeseburgers and fries. When they got their food, they sat down at a table and Angie said the blessing.

"We're worried Mom," Amy uttered.

"So am I Amy," Angie told her.

"Yeah Mom, I'm worried too," Bryon told her.

"You've grown to love them too huh?" Angie inquired.

"Yes I love them Mom. I never thought we'd be without them," said Bryon near to tears.

"I love them too Momma," Amy stated.

"I just hope we can get them back soon," she mentioned.

"Who you think took them?" Bryon asked.

"I think their mother's people took them. I think I'm right," she told them.

"Why?" Amy asked confused.

"Because I took them away from her and the law put her in jail. Some people want revenge any way they can get it," she told them.

"Yeah, but what you did was legal. She had no right to treat them like that. I felt sorry for them," Bryon explained.

"Up until now they were happy Mom," Amy said.

"What you gonna do?" asked Bryon.

"Go after them if I have to," she stated.

"Really?" Bryon asked surprised.

"Yes of course. I wouldn't hesitate a second to go after you. I wouldn't have a chance if Ralph hadn't given me custody. I don't know if Maggie knew about it or not," she told them.

"Who's Maggie?" Amy asked.

"Their mother," she answered.

"Wasn't she on drugs heavy?" Bryon asked.

"Yes she did, she won't have any now," she stated.

"What do you mean?" Amy asked.

"She'll get the drugs out of her system in jail," she answered.

"Oh okay," Amy uttered.

"If she had them taken away from us, she deserves to pay big time," Bryon stated.

"Let the law do their job. I'm sure Judge Russell will do the right thing," she told them.

"What if they can't find them?" Amy asked.

"I hope they will. I just hope they didn't lie to Miss Teasdale," Angie said very worried.

"They'd be in big trouble if they did," Bryon uttered. "Right Mom?"

"Yes the law will deal with them sooner or later," Angie, said.

"Why do you think their mother's people had something to do with this?" he asked.

"Sometimes revenge can be powerful. If Maggie thinks, I don't have custody she'll have them taken away. They'll have to answer to God in the end for their actions. That's when they'll really have to pay," she explained.

"Really?" Bryon asked surprised.

"Yes of course, remember that. If you're finished eating let's go. We've been here for two hours," she said.

"Okay Mom, I'm ready," said Bryon.

"Me too Mom," Amy mentioned.

When they got back to the sheriff's office, they found Burt on the telephone. They sat down to wait until he finished. Several minutes later, he saw them sitting by the door.

"Well Mrs. Bradshaw, I've got good news for you and bad news. They caught them at a roadblock on the outside of town. A female officer is taking care of the children. The bad news is that they won't be able to bring them down here for three days," he explained.

"Call them back and tell them I'm on my way to get them. I have the papers I signed from Judge Russell in my purse. You'll have to write down how I'm supposed to get there," she told him.

"Okay, let me call them back," he said.

Several minutes later, he came back to the counter and motioned for them to come up. He took his cap off and ruffled up his hair.

"You got a cell phone?" he asked.

"Yes sir, but I don't use it much," she answered.

He handed her a folded piece of paper. Angie unfolded it and looked at it a moment. She wondered what this was.

"Call this number when you get close to town and they'll meet you at the sheriff's office. It's a five or six hour drive up there. I told them you'd be leaving right away," he explained.

"Thank you so much," she told him. "They gonna be up in the middle of the night?"

"Yes ma'am, they'll be waiting. Just be careful going up there. There's some hair pin curves in the road," he said.

He wrote down a set of directions and then they left the office. She drove careful all the way up there. She did no want to drive fast and have some animal jump out in front of her. There could be a moose or bear standing in the road as she came around a curve. It was a long trip as the headlights lit up the road in front of her.

At two o'clock in the morning she woke up Bryon and had him dial the number Burt gave her. She was a little frustrated because this trip was taking too long.

"Hello," a woman's voice said.

"I'm Angie Bradshaw. Burt Johnson told me to call when I got close to town. We're about four miles out," she told her.

"Oh yes," she uttered. "You know where the police station's at?"

"No ma'am," she answered.

"The sheriff's office and the police station's in the same building. When you come up Main Street you'll see a blue sign showing you the way," she explained.

"Okay, thank you," Angie, said.

Several minutes later, she stopped in front of the building. Angie and her children walked inside not sure where to go. She started to get worried when she could not see Jenny and Jason. She found the sheriff's office to the left and then she saw a young man sitting in a small office. He looked up as they stopped near the desk.

"Yes ma'am, can I help you?" he asked.

"I'm here to pick up my children. If you have any questions this paper shows that I have full custody of them," she told him.

"Ain't you from Hagon's Bluff?" he asked.

"Yes sir," she answered. "Where are they?"

"They'll be here in about five minutes," he mentioned.

"Thank you," she said.

Angie stepped out of the office and stood in the doorway as she could watch the front door. Each minute dragged by for her feeling like an hour. Several minutes later, she heard the front door open. She stood with her heart in her throat making her unmovable. It could be anyone coming in. When Jenny and Jason saw her, they ran to her as hard as they could hollering "Momma" loudly several times. Angie held her arms out and Jenny and Jason ran into them almost knocking her over.

The female officer walked up a minute later and stood giggling as she watched them. Angie clung to them in desperation as tears flowed down her cheeks. A couple of uncontrolled sobs came out as she held them. The female officer was amazed because she had not seen children act this way for a long time.

"There's no mistaking who you are. You're all they talked about since they heard you was coming to get them. You need to sign a release form and then you're free to go," she told Angie.

"Yes ma'am, I've been through a lot with them. I went through a lot to get them. Thank you so much. I just hope that the one's that took them are locked up," she said sternly.

"You're welcome ma'am. Yes they're in custody," she told her.

"Let me sign them out and then we're going home," she said.

"Can I make a copy of your custody paper for out files please?" the young man asked.

"Yes sir," she answered taking out the paper.

It took him a couple of minutes to make copies of her papers, and then he handed them back to her.

"Thank you so much ma'am. This will help a great deal when this goes to court," he said.

"You're welcome, glad to help," she told him.

"We was scared Momma, we didn't know where they was taking us," Jenny told her.

"I know, I was scared too," she agreed.

"Here you go ma'am. Sign there on the line ma'am," she said.

Angie signed the paper. It was a standard release form. While Angie was signing the paper, Bryon and Amy hugged Jenny and Jason. Now they knew beyond a doubt that they were part of Angie's family. Yes, they belonged in every way. They were happier now than they had ever been before.

They went out to the car and got in. While Angie was driving out of town, she remembered seeing a truck stop after the next town. An hour and a half later, she parked the car and they went inside. They sat down at a table and soon the waitress came over to take their order. They placed their order and then the waitress left to go to the kitchen.

"Who took you away?" Angie asked.

"They told us they were our Aunt and Uncle but we don't remember seeing them before," Jenny told her.

"Tell her about our mother," Jason said.

"Oh yes, they said our mother gave them custody of us. That's why they came and got us. She didn't know what Dad done," Jenny told her.

"Did you tell them?" Angie asked.

"No, we never thought about it. They told us they'd beat us if we didn't shut up so we just sat there. As we was coming into town, the road was blocked with cop cars. We thought we was never going to see you again Momma," Jenny explained as she started crying again.

"You're safe now with us. We love you very much. We never want anything to happen to you," Angie told them.

"I love you Momma," Jenny said.

"I love you," she proudly told them.

"Me too," Jason said.

"I love you too Jason," Angie told him smiling. "You think it was some of your mother's relation?"

"I don't know," Jenny replied.

"When your father gets back we'll find out," Angie stated.

"We have to go to school today?" Amy asked.

"No, school will be started by the time we get back," she answered.

"When can we have a pony Mom?" Amy asked.

Angie rolled her eyes and then she looked at Amy. That was a huge responsibility taking care of a large animal. She knew horses were nice to have but a person could get hurt also. She did not want anyone hurt.

"We'd have to put up a fence, buy hay bales, buy horse feed, build a shed, and feed it everyday," Angie told her. "Who'd take care of the horse?"

"We would," Amy, answered quickly.

"Who'd take care of the animal when it got sick?" Angie asked.

"I don't know, call a doctor," Amy replied.

"What kind of doctor would take care of a horse?" Angie inquired.

"A horse doctor," Amy answered.

"Oh brother," Bryon uttered looking away.

"A veterinarian take care of animals," Angie said. "Will you think about it some?"

"I'd still like to have one," Amy insisted.

"We'll talk about it later. As soon as we get done eating, we're going home. I'm ready to go to bed," she told them.

A half an hour later, they left to go home. At a few minutes until ten in the morning, they arrived at home very tired. Everyone took showers and went to bed. Before Angie went to bed, she called the school to inform them that her children would not be in school today.

About three o'clock that afternoon Angie got up and made a pot of coffee. She never wanted to go through this sort of thing again. She had trouble sleeping as the past twenty-four hours was constantly on her mind. Who were those people? A few minutes later, the phone rang and she picked up the receiver.

"Hello," said Angie.

"I've got your car sold Mrs. Bradshaw. I'll be over in the morning to get it out of the barn. They'll be down here in a week," Ben told her. "You want me to get it cleaned up and running?"

"Yes please. I've got to take the kids to school and I'll make sure it's unlocked," she told him.

"Okay, thank you Mrs. Bradshaw," Ben said.

"You're welcome," she uttered.

She learned so far that he could be trusted. She had no idea herself about the price of old cars. She just hoped that he would treat her right.

It was good to be home. This had been a heart-wrenching experience. When all of the children got up, they went to town to get something to eat. This would be the first time they went to eat in Hagon's Bluff. She parked the car, they went inside, and sat down at a table. Bryon took a chair from a nearby table so he could sit down with all of them.

Soon a woman in her thirties came over to take their order. She looked at the children several times and then looked at Angie. She was trying to put a hunch together but she was not sure what it was She knew that she had seen the Thompkin's children before. She started to speak, and then changed her mind for a moment. She did not want to be too bold in what she said.

"By any chance are you Angie Bradshaw?" she asked unsure.

"Yes I am," she answered.

"I thought it was you. If there's anything I can do for you let me know. I wish I could be like you. You're such a strong woman. That's a wonderful thing you did for those children," she told her.

"Why thank you," Angie uttered.

"You're welcome to come to our club in town. It's a cross between a garden club and a decorating club. That way you'd meet some of the women in town," she suggested.

"It sounds interesting," Angie said.

"My name's Abby McCormick," she told her.

"It's so nice to meet you. Come over some time," Angie suggested.

"I will, I will. I'll be back in a minute," Abby told her.

Things were coming together nicely. She was making friends, had all of her inheritance taxes paid, and now Ben had one of the cars sold. Hopefully, that will keep her out of debt for a while. The only bills she had now were the utilities, and they were not much.

"Okay, I'm back," Abby announced. "Did you inherit that place?"

"Yes I did, it's been a challenge," Angie answered.

"What about all of these children?" she asked.

"I gave birth to Bryon and Amy. I have full custody of Jennie and Jason. Three of them are twelve, and Amy's ten," Angie told her.

"They're all so well mannered and good looking. I can't say the boys are pretty because it wouldn't be right. My kids are eight, ten, and twelve. I don't want any more. Let me see if your order's ready," she told her.

Ten minutes later, she came back with their food. She sat the plates on the table and then she left to bring back the coffee pot. She kept watching from the kitchen and when she saw that Angie finished eating Abby went over to their table.

"How was your food?" she asked.

"Very good, thank you," Angie told her.

"He's young but he does okay," Abby mentioned.

"My phone number is listed under Morgan Bradshaw," she said.

"I'll find it," she uttered. "You married?"

"No, I lost my husband to cancer," Angie said.

"I lost mine in a logging accident. I'm sorry you lost your husband. We live in a dinky apartment.

"I'm sorry you lost your husband. We live in a dinky apartment. This is the only job I could find. I don't know why I'm telling you, it's not interesting. Well anyway to some it's not," Abby, told her.

"We're gonna go, I'll talk to you later," she said.

"Okay take care," Abby, told her.

Angie got up and paid the bill and then they went home to relax. When she took the kids to school in the morning, she wanted to thank Miss Teasdale personally.

10

A week later, Ben called the house early. Angie almost forgot about the car. He sounded excited this morning.

"Hello," she said.

"They'll be here between ten and noon. I'll bring the car over in a little bit," he told her.

"Okay, that'll be fine, I'll be here," she mentioned.

"Thank you Mrs. Bradshaw," he said.

"You're welcome," she replied.

An hour later, he drove the car over and parked it in front of the garage. Angie walked out as he came up. She could not believe her eyes.

"That's my car?" she inquired overwhelmed.

"Yes ma'am," he answered.

"You did a great job, it really looks good," she uttered. "Did you get a good price?"

"Yes, you'll be surprised," he answered.

"It's a secret huh?" she asked.

"No, but I want him to tell you," he told her.

"Okay," she said skeptically. "It run good?"

"Yes ma'am, come here and listen," he told her.

She walked over to the car with him. Ben got in the car and started the engine. It sat there and ran quietly.

"I'm amazed," she uttered. "Are they coming here or to your garage?"

"Here, there's more room here to turn around," he answered.

"That's fine," she agreed. "You know anyone around here that does odd jobs that's dependable and trustworthy?"

"Yeah, there's two boys that work part time at the sawmill. They'll be glad to have something to do," he answered.

"They don't do drugs or drink do they?" she inquired.

"No ma'am," he assured her.

"I want to build a fence around five or ten acres. Then I want to put up a screened in shed that I can have cookouts in. That way I won't have to fight the bugs," she explained.

"They can do that," he agreed.

"Call them for me. Those girls been hounding me about a pony. I need a shed for the pony," she told him.

"Yeah, I know how that goes. I've got three head of youngins'. Each one wants something expensive. Usually more than I can afford. The next thing they'll want is a car," he told her. "Where does it all end?"

"I don't know, I ain't got that far yet," she uttered.

"You will Mrs. Bradshaw," he assured her.

"That's what I'm afraid of," she muttered.

"That looks like them coming now," he said.

A one-ton Chevy truck turned off the highway pulling a long trailer. It came slowly up the driveway and stopped in front of the house.

"We at the right place?" a man asked.

"I hope so," Ben remarked.

"We came about the car there," he said pointing.

"You're at the right place. I'm the one you talked to," Ben told him.

The man and a woman got out of the truck, and Ben and Angie shook hands with them as they introduced themselves.

"Wanna take it for a spin?" Ben asked.

"It runs?" the man asked surprised.

"Yes sir. I cleaned it up a little, put in a fuel pump, a battery, changed the oil and filter, and put in fresh gas. That's all I did to it," he explained.

"The man got in the car and started the engine. Then he backed the car out and drove it down the lane. He drove it down to the highway, and then he drove back. As he parked the car, he was smiling. He shut the engine off and got out.

"Mrs. Bradshaw, I'm well pleased. You'll get a check in the mail for more than I agreed on I agreed on a car. I didn't know if it ran or not. This car runs very good. All I have to do is paint it, fix the upholstery, and take it to shows," he explained.

"You go to a lot of shows?" Ben asked.

"Usually eight or ten a year," he answered.

"I hope you'll enjoy it," Angie said.

"Oh we will," his wife said.

"Where do you live?" Angie asked.

"In New York state. We're Wade and Hazel Townsend. We'll give you our address and phone number. You could come up in the spring. We'll have a cookout when you come. We'd love to have you," Hazel told her.

"What year of car is it?" Angie asked. "I don't know anything about such things."

"It's a nineteen forty-six four door sedan. It's got a six cylinder in line engine. It runs good and it's in excellent shape," Wade told her. "How long have you had it?"

"I inherited it and two more cars," she said. "Would you like to take a look?"

"Yes we would," Hazel, answered.

"Come on, they're out in the barn," Angie told them.

They followed her out to the barn and she unlocked the door. Wade and Ben took the tarps off the other two cars.

"Oh, I like this one," Hazel uttered.

"I hate to sound stupid or something," Angie stated. "What year is it?"

"It's a nineteen thirty-six Lafayette," he answered. "Does it run?"

"I have no idea," Angie answered.

"We can get it running, but getting the parts may take a while," Ben said.

"We're in no hurry before spring," Wade mentioned.

"I could bring it to you," Angie suggested.

"That'd be excellent," Hazel, uttered.

"Hey wait a minute," Angie said suddenly. "What am I gonna do with my kids?"

"How many you got?" Hazel asked surprised.

"I've got four. I was going to borrow Ben's truck," she answered.

"I'll drive the truck up there for you," Ben suggested.

Hazel looked around inside the car checking every detail. Several minutes later, she got out and closed the door.

"I like this car Wade. I haven't seen one before," she told him.

"I've seen a picture of one," he mentioned.

Hazel opened her purse, took out an envelope, and handed it to Angie. Then Hazel walked to the other car. Angie followed along to find out what they thought.

"Here's the title to the car," Angie said.

"Oh thank you so much," Hazel told her.

"What's the other car Ben?" Angie asked.

"A Model "A"," he answered. "You know anyone that want's to buy it?"

"A friend of ours might take it. He likes those cars," he answered.

Ben helped them load the car on the trailer and then they chained it down. They checked the trailers tires and lights. Everything checked out all right.

"It was so nice to meet you. We're going to head out. It's a long ride back home," Wade told her.

They shook hands with Angie, and then they got in the truck. Angie and Ben stood and watched them go up the lane.

"How much do I owe you Ben?" she asked.

"I spent eighty dollars in parts," he answered.

"Okay, I'll bring it to you in the morning. Thank you so much for getting it ready," she said.

"You're welcome Mrs. Bradshaw," he told her. "Can you take me to the garage?"

"Oh yes of course. Stay with the others Bryon, I'll be back in ten minutes," she said.

"Okay Mom," he told her nodding his head.

She took Ben back to the garage and dropped him off. On the way back, she opened the envelope as she drove. Inside was a certified check for twenty-five thousand. She almost slammed on the brakes as she stared at the check. A car came up behind her and honked the horn. She quickly looked in the mirror and then she stepped down on the accelerator pedal.

At home, she walked into the house with a shocked look on her face. She looked at the check again. The numbers had not changed. Wade said that he would send another five thousand to her. She could not get over it, all of that money for an old car. Then she got to thinking to herself. How much was the other one worth if this one was worth this much.

"What is it Mom?" Bryon asked.

She turned the check around and showed it to him. Now Bryon's eyes opened wide.

"That's a lot of money for an old car," he stated.

"Yes I know," she uttered.

"Wow Mom, we're rich!" he exclaimed.

"What is it Mom?" Jenny asked as she came into the room.

"It surprised me how much I got for that old car," she said. "You want a pony too?"

"Oh yes Mom," she answered quickly.

"Okay we'll work on that," she told her.

"Really?" she asked not believing her ears.

"Yes of course Jenny," she said as she smiled.

She ran off to find Amy to tell her the good news. She was very excited because each of them would get a pony to ride.

"There'll be two men coming over to put up a barbed wire fence and a shed. Then they're going to put up a cookhouse," she told him.

"A cookhouse?" he asked confused.

"Yeah, so we can have cookouts without fighting bugs," she answered. "You think we ought to keep the other car?"

"What is it?" he asked.

"A Model "A" Ford," she answered.

"Does it have a rear seat in the trunk?" Bryon asked.

"I guess, I don't know about such things. In three years you'll be old enough to drive a car, only I have to ride with you," she told him.

"Yeah I know," he uttered.

"You'll be all grown up soon," she reminded him.

"Mom!" he exclaimed.

"Me too Mom," Jason said.

"Yes, you'll be old enough soon. I'm gonna go out of my mind with three kids old enough to drive at the same time," she uttered.

"It won't be that bad Mom," Bryon said.

"You sure?" she asked.

"Yes Mom," he answered.

"Well if I'm gonna get the girls ponies, I've been thinking about getting you go carts or something," she suggested.

"Yes Mom, that'd be neat. A four wheeler would be better," Bryon, told her.

"Yeah Mom," Jason chimed in.

"They cost a lot of money. We'll start with go-carts. I've got to save so all of you can go to college," she told them.

"Okay, we can handle that," Bryon uttered. "When can we go exploring?"

"I don't know. I need to get boots for all of you. Tennis shoes won't work to hike in. Boots will protect you," she explained.

"Okay," they agreed.

"What's those girls doing?" Angie asked.

"I don't know, they're girls," Bryon stated.

"You won't think that in a few years. You won't be able to live without a girl," she told him.

"What do you mean?" he asked.

"You'll have deep feelings for a girl," she said.

"I don't know about that," Jason remarked.

"That's a long ways away," Bryon mentioned.

"Yeah, a long ways," Jason added.

Angie chuckled at the boys. Their feelings would change sooner than they thought. They could surprise her. Jenny and Jason had come a long ways in a few months. The grades on their last report card were fair. Both of them almost failed English. Bryon and Amy had real good grades.

The next morning she went to the bank to deposit the check. Then she drove to Ben's garage.

"Good morning Mrs. Bradshaw," he said cheerfully.

"Good morning," she told him.

She handed him five one hundred dollar bills. He stood looking at the money for a moment.

"You didn't have to do that Mrs. Bradshaw," he stammered.

"Yes I did. It cost you to make phone calls and it'll give you an incentive to get the other car running. The sooner you get started the better off we'll be," she told him.

"Yes ma'am, I'll come and get it tomorrow," he said.

"Okay, thank you," she told him.

"Thank you Mrs. Bradshaw," he stated.

"I'll see you tomorrow," she told him.

"Okay," he uttered.

The two men came and put up a fence with a metal gate. Then they built a ten by twenty shed with a big doorway. When they finished that, they talked to Angie about the cookhouse. A cement floor had to be poured with reinforcement steel.

Four weeks later, the kids brought their report cards home. Bryon and Amy's grades were a little higher. Jenny and Jason's grades made a big improvement. Jason had one A and one C, and the rest was in between.

"I'm so proud of all of you. You worked hard to bring your grades up," she told them excitedly.

"Thank you Mom," all of them said.

"I try," Jason stammered.

"Yes, you did more than try," she said sincerely. "What's today?"

"Thursday," Jenny quickly answered.

"All right, Saturday morning is yours," she told them. "What do you want to do?"

"I don't know Mom," Bryon said.

"There's a skating rink in Tabor's Point," she suggested.

"Oh yeah," Amy uttered. "Can we Mom?"

"Yes of course," she answered.

Jason still stammered over his words when he got excited. Angie kept his hair neatly trimmed on the sides and about two inches long on top. Jenny's hair hung four inches below the top of her shoulders. She kept it brushed everyday. Angie was thankful that Bryon and Jason wore their clothes neatly and not bagging off their back side like some of the kids at school. When she first came here, her life was not easy. Jason rebelled about many things and Jenny would go into silent mode. With the overbearing love she show them, they changed. She did not know what she would have done if Bryon and Amy had not accepted Jenny and Jason at first.

"Mom, there's something we want to say," Bryon said.

"Yes, what is it?" she asked.

"We love you Mom," all four of them hollered out.